The Man Who Lived On The Moon

The Man Who Lived On The Moon

by

Peter Basham

Published by

Peter & Elizabeth Basham

First published in Great Britain in 2015
by Peter and Elizabeth Basham

Copyright © Text and Illustrations
Peter and Elizabeth Basham 2015

All rights reserved. This book, or any portion thereof, may not be reproduced or used in any manner whatsoever, without the express written permission of the publisher and copyright owner.

ISBN 978-0-9934341-0-5

Printed in Great Britain by
Berforts Group Ltd. Stevenage.

My heartfelt thanks
to all who have helped make this
story a reality;
especially my imaginary friends.

Chapter 1
Eva Verity Briggs

The man on the moon, does he whistle a tune,
when he eats the cheese, that rests on his knees?
I wonder what sort, and how is it caught?
Why are there no taters, among the moon's craters,
baked by the sun, now that would be fun,
with lashings of cheese, how that would please.
It's made from the milk, smooth as silk,
obtained from the cow, I wonder how,
as it leaps overhead. Is it well fed?
It must be a boon, for the man who lives on the moon.

Eva Verity Briggs was five years old and tall for her age. One of her most favourite things was listening to the soft, singsong tones of her mother's voice, as it spoke her favourite story; the one about the man who lived on the moon. The flow of her mother's words settled into a rhythm, which matched the brushstrokes, as she brushed Eva's nut-brown hair.

It was a story that Eva never tired of hearing.

'Mummy,' she said, interrupting her mother; 'what happens to the rest of the moon? You know, when it's that cresss...thingy.'

'Well, my little Evie...' began her mother, thinking fast. Joy Briggs always called her daughter, Evie, except when she was naughty, and then it would be, 'Eva Verity Briggs,' in the quiet firm voice she reserved for such occasions. '...you know I told you that the moon is a ball of cheese, made from the milk of the cow who jumped over it. Well, just like you at teatime, the man gets hungry too, and all he has to eat is cheese, which is good for him. So, you see, the moon gets smaller every day, and when he's eaten it all he has to make some more. If you look carefully, from the corner of your eye, you can sometimes catch a glimpse of him dancing on the moonlit surface of a lake, or the sea, or even a puddle; but only when he's finished making his next batch of cheese, and the moon is full again.

Eva kept her mouth shut while she digested this new information. Her bright blue eyes swivelled in the direction of the window, looking past the half-closed dark blue curtains, dotted with colourful stars, out into the night sky, searching for a glimpse of the crescent moon; but it had disappeared behind a thick cloud. The pitter-patter on the glass, told her it had begun to rain.

Her mother, sensing another but, forming on Eva's lips, quickly continued with her explanation. 'You know I showed you that caterpillar, the one who eats the cabbage leaves on the vegetable patch; the way it starts eating at the edge and nibbles...'

'In a round way,' Eva cut in, her finger tracing a crescent in the air, her mouth mimicking a nibbling action, as she pretended to be a caterpillar.

'That's right. Well the man on the moon eats the cheese in the same way.'

'Is he a caterpillar?'

Joy Briggs chuckled loudly. 'No, no, a caterpillar is one step away from becoming a butterfly. The man on the moon is...like you and me.'

'Don't be silly, mummy. He's a man; we're girls.'

Her mother smiled in agreement and not for the first time,

and definitely not the last, marvelled at the way her daughters mind worked. She supposed that even for a five year old, Eva's imagination was extremely active; something she positively encouraged. She remembered her own mother telling her that she was the same at that age.

'How does the cow jump over the moon?' Eva suddenly asked. 'Daddy said it's a long way away.'

'Evie, I think it time you settled down and went to sleep,' her mother said. 'It's a big day tomorrow; first day at school.'

Eva pulled a face, which transformed into a sleepy yawn, as she climbed under the bedclothes.

Her mother leaned over and kissed her on the cheek, before whispering in her ear, 'it's the cat who plays the fiddle that makes the cow jump over the moon.'

'It must be magic music,' Eva said sleepily.

'Oh no, it isn't, quite the contrary. Every month, the cat sneaks up on a cow and starts playing his fiddle. He plays it really badly; the screeching, scraping sound he makes hardly resembles a tune. It makes the cow jump as high as high can be. That's how the man gets the milk to make his cheese.'

Eva yawned, saying, 'Cheese is good. I like cheese, mummy; it's got calci-something in it; you said it's good for my bones, because I'm only five and need to grow. Mummy, will I grow as big as daddy? He's stopped growing, even though he still eats lots of cheese. You're still growing, mummy, so you'd better eat more cheese.'

Her mother laughed, as she patted the small bump that was beginning to show on her stomach. 'Go to sleep, my little Evie,' she said, 'you'll grow bigger soon enough.'

Eva glanced at the window. The moon was trying desperately to shine its light through a gap in the thickening cloud, and for an instant, before her mother drew the curtains, she thought she saw the man snuggling into the curve of the crescent moon. A silver and gold moonbeam squeezed through a chink in the curtains, settling on her forehead, and melting into her mind, to skip and play on the ocean of her imagination. She closed her eyes and drifted into a deep sleep, full of dreams about a white and black cow, a mischievous cat, a badly played fiddle, but most of all about her best imaginary friend, the man who lived on the moon; with twinkling stars of red and gold, green and silver, peppering the sky above his tall stovepipe hat.

Chapter 2

There is a Moon on My World, Too

My name is Sessil, and there is a moon on my world, too; perhaps that's why I'm now continually watching yours, always waiting for a glimpse through its window, looking for the way back home to my world.

There are many stories about the moon on my world, as there are here, of how it affects people. Some profess that its light instils a feeling of melancholy. Myself, well I've always loved its light, whether it's the cool silver face it shows, or one with the golden glow. I love the colours in its aura, shining through the veiled curtain of cloud. On my world, night was the time for work, the hot days for sleeping.

My father told me one story about a man who lived on our moon, that he was the one who turned its light off at the end of its cycle, and on again at the start of the new one. However, the story that keeps coming into my mind stems from an age when time still existed for us.

The story told us that the moon is a window into other worlds, and from it, we're able to see how they fare on their paths of evolution. Long ago, scientists observed many strange and wonderful places, and concluded that the life existing on each world, stemmed from the same source.

The story said that at the end of the moon's cycle, when it's at its fullest and fattest, it sends out threads of light, almost undetectable to the naked eye. Those lucky few, or should I say those with heightened awareness, know where to look; not at the moon's full face, but to its edges, where you can see these moonbeams as they begin to seek out other worlds. Call them wormholes, light beams, or simply windows; each resonates at a different frequency, which gives them a unique colour, the key to opening windows of the same colour onto other worlds.

On our world there lived a young boy, with an over active imagination, coupled with an insatiable curiosity. He wished with all his heart for a glimpse of these other worlds.

One day, his wish was granted, in a way he didn't expect. Let me explain how.

One clear night, when the heavens were at their best, showing a multitude of stars, the boy sat beside a pond, watching the golden colours of moonlight as they sang and danced upon the water. He screwed his face up with concentration, and wished with all his might that he could climb the moonbeam to its source, and look through its window at other worlds.

'Are you sure it's what you want?' A deep and earthy voice reverberated in his head. 'Well. What is your answer?' the voice asked, a little impatiently this time, as the ground rumbled and thumped like it was tapping its foot as it waited for an answer.

The boys head spun around, but there was no one there. 'Yes,' he eventually replied, a little anxiously. Tightness gripped his stomach, his jacket ballooned out in front of him, and the next second he was on the moon and tumbling through the window.

He was never seen again; but it's said that when the moon is full, if you sneak a look out of the corner of your eye, you might catch a ghostly glimpse of him, skipping across the moonlit surface of a lake, an ocean, or even a puddle, searching for the right moonbeam that will bring him home.

How appropriate to my situation. Perhaps that's why this story looms large in my imagination. Maybe I'll be like him; never to be seen again on my world.

Chapter 3

First Sight of the Sea

Joy Briggs studied Eva, as her daughter stared and stared at the endless, moving mass of water, as it frothed and foamed on golden sand; her face was alive with excitement.

Through her daughter, Joy relived the moment when her parents had taken her to the coast for the first time, and she too had set eyes on the vast expanse of sea and sand. She'd been the same age as Eva; nearly six years old.

She'd told Eva the story many times; how the smell of the sea, caught by a sea breeze, wafted through the dunes, to be ready and waiting in the car park, just for her; the salty tang clinging to her tongue, seagulls, with their raucous cries circling overhead. It had been all her father could do to stop her rushing to the wide sandy beach that lay beyond the dunes. Now it was her daughters turn to feel the thrill and anticipation of the sight, sound and smell of the sea.

Eva's mouth hung open, as she tried to express what she was feeling, her hand clutching her mother's in a tight grip of exhilaration. It was so much bigger, and better, than anything she'd seen on the television. Excitement welled up inside her, from the pit of her stomach up into her chest, and unable to contain herself, she broke free of her mother's hand, and raced forward onto the beach, the loose sand dragging at her feet, slowing her down.

'Come on, slowcoach,' her father called as he strode past, 'race you to the water.'

'Wait, daddy,' Eva wailed, 'it's not fair, you're bigger than me.'

'Not my fault,' her father called back over his shoulder, just before he feigned a stumble a few yards from the waterline.

Eva laughed as she ran past him, stopping suddenly as cool frothy water washed over her feet. The strong hands of her father scooped her up, and he carried her a little further out into the sea.

'What do you think?' he said, smiling broadly, as he set his daughter down in the water, keeping a tight hold of her hand.

The pull of the tide was strong, and Eva tightened her grip.

'Cool, Daddy,' she managed to say.

'Yes, it is a bit, my toes are getting numb. Let's go find your mother; she's got the bag with the goodies. First one back gets the dark chocolate and mint bar.'

With such incentive, Eva took off as fast as she could to where her mother sat with the prize.

The rest of the day passed happily, with ice cream, sandcastles, football, paddling, and skipping stones on the water. Her father managed three, mother four, in spite of the large bulge of her stomach, which cramped her style. Eva's just plopped, but she didn't mind.

By late afternoon, it was time to leave, and with a last look at the sea, laced with promises of returning the next morning, Eva trudged after her parents, back through the sand dunes, which seemed to have grown much taller since the morning.

Chapter 4

Heaven is a Chocolate Mousse

The little two-up two-down cottage, where they were staying, belonged to a friend of a friend. Once back there, Joy Briggs tidied everything away, and began to think about dinner; but only for a minute or two, before her husband, Henry, suggested going to the cafe down the road. It took only a second for her to agree.

Situated beside a small pond, which stood in as a boating lake, near the entrance of Turnstones Campsite, the cafe offered a surprisingly good menu, with plenty of locally sourced ingredients.

The child's portion of homemade fish fingers, with crispy chips and garden peas, was surprisingly big, and Eva attacked it with gusto. Her parents had the plaice, lightly crumbed and fried in butter, washed down with a glass of freshly squeezed orange juice. As the chocolate mousse that followed melted in her mouth, Eva thought she'd never tasted anything so delicious, but then to a six year old, anything chocolaty is heaven.

'Absolutely scrumptious,' Henry Briggs said, as the waitress appeared to clear away the plates.

'Good. I'll tell old Bob.'

'Who's old Bob?' Eva chirped.

'He owns Turnstones,' the waitress replied. 'He helps out in here when we're busy. The mousse is his recipe.'

'Why do you call him, old?'

'None of your business, Evie,' Henry Briggs said.

'It's all right, sir,' the waitress replied.

'Well he's a good cook,' Eva said, handing the waitress her dish.

She smiled, and winked at Eva. 'I'll tell him,' and she hurried off with the empty dishes.

Eva watched her go through the swing doors into the kitchen. A few minutes later, they swung back open, revealing a figure of an elderly man framed in the doorway, a tall white hat perched precariously on his head. His sad eyes suddenly twinkled with good humour, a friendly smile accentuating the lines on his face as he saw Eva, and waved, just before the waitress squeezed past him, carrying a tray loaded with cups and a pot of coffee for Eva's parents.

She leaned forward and whispered in Eva's ear. 'Bob made this especially for you. He said, as you love dark chocolate, you'd like this. It's his secret recipe. He only makes it for special people,' and she set a mug of hot chocolate in front of her.

After finishing her meal, Eva sat with her parents on a bench outside the cafe, watching a few of the campsite's residents as they hung around the boating lake. Children launched toy yachts. Their sails, caught by a gentle breeze, tacked towards the opposite side, into the waiting hands of their excited, out of breath, launchers. Other youngsters, egged on by their parents into a game of crazy golf, shouted and screamed in tired frustration when their ball missed the clown's mouth, or failed to reach the bottom of the windmill. They'd rather have been playing football, anyway.

The sound of the shutters closing on the cafe windows

scattered the revellers back to their caravans and tents. Old Bob turned the key in the door, and waved to Eva, before setting off around the lake for his evening constitutional. He stopped to look over the water, just as the sky blazed red and gold, before the encroaching twilight.

Eva, who was also watching, thought the sun melted, just like the chocolate mousse had melted on her tongue. Stars blinked into view across the indigo canvas, as night claimed its place on the day. A few brave clouds, in an attempt to hide the full moon, hung like gossamer curtains in the cooling air. Eva, entranced by the colourful aura the moon projected, wished with all her might that she could see the man on the moon. She stared and stared, until her eyelids became too heavy to keep open.

'Come on, Evie, it's late,' her mother cooed. 'Time you were in bed, young lady.'

As Eva climbed from the bench and started to follow her parents, the cloud moved off the moon. From the corner of her eye, she saw the moonlight zigzagging across the surface of the boating lake, and for a fleeting moment, she saw him, the man on the moon, dancing round and round on the ripples of moonlight; only he was small, a child, like her. His illuminated face, though golden and bright, held a sad, melancholy expression, as he spun in circles, oblivious to everything but the moment. He lifted his head, his eyes locking onto Eva's gaze; he smiled a smile, full of longing, brimming with hope, and then he was gone with the moonlight, as a thick, uncaring cloud darkened the sky.

'Come along, slowcoach,' her father called.

'But, dad, it was him,' Eva said, running to catch her parents up.

'Who, dear?' her mother asked.

'The man on the moon, just like you said. He was sad. He must be lonely.'

Her father picked her up, and glancing at his wife, said, 'then when we get home, you must say a little prayer for him. Send him some happiness.'

Chapter 5

A World Away From Home

I came from a world, a universe away, or maybe it was another dimension. I fell from my world, and arrived on that lump of rock, overlooking your world, many revolutions ago.

I was alone, a solitary figure, how I survived, I don't know. It seemed like I'd been sleeping for a long time, or maybe I'd been living in a dream. I was stuck on a little piece of rock that kept its face to the sun, as it moved through the heavens. I existed within the cusp of light and dark, feeding on the warmth of that halfway place, always in shadow, not totally in the dark; and there was my hope. At first, I was frightened, but soon realized that everything that made me who I am was still there: I was alive.

I know none of this makes sense. I learnt that the light and warmth of your sun sustained me, fed me, while I could only worry about my dilemma; how could I get home? Was there even a home waiting for me? How or why I was still alive, I didn't know. Perhaps it's because I kept thinking of my home.

I remembered my name, Sessil, after one of the many species of trees that once populated my world, but I didn't have a body; although I have to admit, that's not strictly true, what I mean is, I wasn't physical. When I held up my hand, and wriggled my fingers, little sparks, like stars, danced from their tips. I could see a faint outline, but it was like I wasn't there.

It seemed one step further away from physicality than it was on my world, where my body was light and airy, semi-solid; it was fused to the colours of my aura. Mine favoured the softer, warmer yellows, but that was because I was young, not fully mature. Other children leaned towards gentle blues, greens, or pinks. As people grew, the colours of their auras evolved into patterns around their body, each one unique; and the lightness of our auras enabled us to fly.

Some would say I had been lucky to be born in the dome of The Heartoak, the last surviving tree of the vast swathe of equatorial forest that used to circumnavigate the equator of our world. It reached a thousand feet into the sky. How no one had seen it before the death of the forest, I can't say. My father said it was a case of not seeing the tree for the forest.

The Heartoak was the last vestige of hope for my world; and it turned out to be the instrument that brought me here. The soul of my world was using The Heartoak to broadcast pleas for help. Using the moon's beams to send out messages into space, the tree reached out to the farthest corners of the universe, and beyond, even as my species of man rushed towards the edge of the abyss that held our destruction; such was the love our world held for us.

My parents were caretakers of The Heartoak, scientists, who took me everywhere with them. They were working high up in the tree, monitoring the strange, excitable readings emanating from the uppermost branches.

It was a bright, starless night, the moon was full, and I was ensconced in the lower branches of The Heartoak, happily nightdreaming, on your world, it's called daydreaming. Moonlight, reflecting off some of the tree's seeds, reminded me of the story of the boy who dropped through the window on the moon. My imagination took flight, and like him, I too wished with all my heart for a glimpse into those other worlds.

I crawled to the end of the branch, intent on securing a seed, thinking it'd hold the secret of moonlight. That's when it happened; my fingers closed around a clump of acorns, just as one of the thin snakelike threads of vibration, a bright yellow one, wrapped itself around my wrist. The last thing I remember was seeing my father's look of terror, as he grasped franticly at the air as I whipped past, my mother, screaming beside him.

My wish had come true; I found myself at the window on the moon, and as I fell through, had second thoughts, but it was too late. I grabbed for something to hold on to, jarring my body on the edge of the window. Darkness clouded my vision.

I vividly remember a tickly sensation, like pins and needles all over my body, and then everything went black.

I woke up looking at your world; the blue oceans, the green

lands, the swirling moist clouds of the Earth. I'd never seen anything so colourful. My world paled, compared to the Earth.

Chapter 6
Eva's Journal

Henry Briggs encouraged his daughters growing interest in the moon, and fed her with all sorts of facts, about its size, distance from Earth, how its eccentric orbit affected the world's oceans; pretty boring stuff for a growing child, who took in only a few of the facts, and understood even less.

Eva's father believed in the pursuit of knowledge, but also in the truth of imagination, and so reinforced the stories about the man on the moon. You might think this is contradictory, and would pull Eva both ways, fact or fiction, confusing her young mind with what is real and what is just a story; it didn't. Both Henry and Joy believed that stories fed the imagination, and imagination did the same for curiosity, which, in turn, sought out truth.

With the arrival of Felicity, a small bundle of screaming baby sister, Eva was left more to her own devices, to dream of the man on the moon, while her parents went through all the motions of a new baby. It seemed to Eva to be a nonstop round of feed, change, sleep.

For her seventh birthday, Eva's father brought home a telescope, which he set up at the window of her bedroom. She had pestered for one after seeing a television programme about the night sky, and finding one in a second-hand shop, Henry had taken it to the college where he worked and spent all his lunch hours cleaning it up.

The first time Eva looked through the eyepiece, the moon looked enormous, and she'd quickly taken her eye away to make sure the moon wasn't crashing towards the window. It'd make a mess, or so she reasoned.

Her father chuckled when she voiced her concern; he then proceeded to explain all about the telescope. It used the reflector system, where light bounced off a curved mirror onto a flat mirror and into the eyepiece. Words such as Newtonian reflecting, parabolic concave, primary and secondary, simply floated over her head, evaporating into a meaningless vapour when compared to the golden face of the moon.

As Eva grew, her curiosity knew no bounds. She'd even been writing a sort of diary; not every day, most days were, after all, mundane; get up, go to school, eat, sleep, pester her mum for sweets, especially chocolate.

In the beginning, Eva's, let's call it, journal, just voiced her thoughts in the most simplistic way. She was a child, and entries went something like...Felicity was sick over my best dress again, then she scribbled in my book and pulled the leg off my teddy bear. Hope mum can mend him...and...I'm sure I saw him, the man on the moon. He was dancing on the birdbath. He didn't empty it like the sparrows and starlings do when they get in. Mum's always telling me to fill it up, when Felis gets older, I'll tell her to do it.

Entries started to become a bit more complex, and after a few months, drawings had begun to take precedence. There was a picture of the moon, which she'd drawn by pencilling around the bottom of a glass. Crayoned in soft yellows, with bands of reds, blues and greens surrounding it; there were little white stars decorating the dark navy background, as she'd run out of black crayon. She drew a face upon the moon, yellow eyes and yellow lips. Underneath, she'd written...yellow, just like the cheese he eats. Bet it's cheddar. Mum says that's the most popular cheese, she buys it all the time. Don't like the funny stuff with blue lines in it that mum buys for a special treat. Dad eats most of it...or...I hope I see him again, the man on the moon.

A few days later, she'd written...Dad says there's no atsmo...air to breathe on the moon. I asked him why the man doesn't move here to Earth. He could live with us, he's only small, because the moon isn't very big, not when I look at it without the telescope. Dad says it looks small because it's a long way away, and maybe that's why the man can't come here very often.

Later that evening she wrote...I dreamt of the moon, the man was crying, and I woke in the middle of the night. I jumped out of bed and looked out of the window hoping to see him, but it was raining.

The next day, Eva nearly drove her father mad, with an endless stream of questions, such as...Where did the moon go? Was the man really eating it all? Where did he go when it wasn't there? How did he make the cheese? Why couldn't she see the cow as it jumped over the moon?

All the time her thoughts reached out to him. She wrote...He must be lonely. I wish he'd answer me, but dad says the moon is over 200,000 miles from Earth, and that's a long, long way away. He said, imagine how long it took me to walk to the park, and that was only half a mile. I tried to work it out, but I haven't got enough fingers. Dad let me use his special calculator, the electric one, with all the buttons and weird symbols. I gave up in the end; it'd probably be years...and...Yesterday, dad said that light travels very fast, so it can't be heavy, not like Mr Turnbull who lives across the road. It's faster than an aeroplane, and they go fast, I've seen them flying over our house. Our dog, Patch, barks every time he sees one, and runs round in circles. He even barks at the moon. I wonder if he sees the man. He barks at the postman, and he's a man.

After that entry, the journal turned into a scrapbook of drawings. There were several about the man on the moon and the cow who jumped over it, some involving Patch, or the chickens next door.

In the evening, before bedtime, Eva would sit at the table, watched by her mother, who listened to her telling a story as she pencilled and crayoned, or felt-tipped her latest picture.

Of course, Eva now knew the moon wasn't really made of cheese, but she still believed with all her soul that the man on the moon was real; she'd seen him.

Later, as she lay in bed, her mother would tell her a story, until her eyes gently closed and she drifted off to sleep.

Chapter 7

Down to Earth

How long I was stranded on the moon, I don't know; I had no sense of time. The Earth's cycles around its sun made no sense to me; it was a timeless existence, at least it was until...

I must've just woken up, although I didn't know I'd even been asleep. I was shivering, the half-light was darkening; fear gripped me. I held out my arms in a vain attempt to push the darkness away. It was odd, my arms looked solid, not translucent like they'd been ever since I landed on the moon, and I felt heavy.

'This must be the end,' I said to no one; who was there to listen. I watched as a shadow began blotting out the sun. The Earth grew darker as it came between the sun and the moon; all colour faded, its rounded edge a stark, flat silhouette that seemed to cut out the light. As the spectacle reached its zenith, a colourful corona formed around the Earth, and a multitude of sunbeams speared into space.

A movement drew my eyes to the centre of the eclipse; from my position, I couldn't tell what it was. At first it looked like a speck of black; well, it was blacker than black, and it was heading straight towards me. As it drew closer, the light from the corona created by the silhouette of the Earth, touched it, revealing its true identity.

It was actually a sphere of swirling colours, trailing behind it, a tail of rich greens and blues, which reminded me of the colours of the Earth. The sphere halted in front of me. A crackling, high-pitched whistling noise emanated from inside, like a radio, searching for the best reception, until a voice sounded, pitch perfect, singing a rhyme...

> *The man on the moon, I can hear his tune,*
> *as he drops to the sea, close to where I'll be.*
> *I'll wait on the sand, ready to take his hand...*

I reached out and gently took hold of the sphere. The next thing I remember was the cold of the water as I splashed into the sea, quickly sinking beneath its dark, moving mass, before bobbing up to the surface. I gasped for air. I tried hauling myself up onto a wave, but found I couldn't fly, like I could on my world. I was so heavy. I sank once again beneath the moonlit water. My strength dissolved in my struggle; it was the end.

Suddenly, hands caught hold of me, a voice whispered in my ear; 'relax, allow me to do the work.' As soon as I relaxed, I felt lighter. I was floating. After a few minutes, my feet touched solid ground, but as I stepped onto a pebbly shore, I toppled over, unable to keep upright. I felt something soft drape around my shoulder; a gentle voice sang...

Man on the moon, I knew you'd come soon.

Take my hand, as we stand on the strand...

'Come on, son,' a deeper voice interrupted, as I struggled to rise. 'It's the gravity; it'll take a while for you to get used to the heaviness of this Earth. What's your name?'

'I-I-I d-d-don't remember,' I stuttered, shivering with effort, as I hauled myself to my feet.

'Perhaps we should call you, Sandy, after the beach we found you on,' said the soft voice.

The deeper voice chuckled, 'very funny, Di. Perhaps it's better to let him chose, later.'

'Yes, Perry, plenty of time for that,' the woman answered.

I swayed uncontrollably, my legs threatening to buckle, but strong arms steadied me. I looked at my hands; they were solid and fleshy. I felt the weight of the soft fleecy blanket the woman had placed around my shoulders, and could tell by the feel of its soft fibres that the rest of my body was also solid. I turned my head towards her, and looked into her deep, amber eyes.

'Who am I?' I asked. My voice sounded thin and childlike, it suited me; I was, after all, a child. I felt lost and alone. I glanced up at the moon; questions tumbling into my mind.

As if reading my thoughts, the woman took my hand in hers and pushed something into it. I looked down to see five acorns sitting in my palm. 'You brought them with you,' she said, small lines crinkling the skin around her eyes as she smiled reassuringly. 'We're like you, stuck here. It's not so bad once you get used to it,' she added, with a sigh. 'My name is Diana...Diana Shaw.'

'And I'm Perry.'

'How did you...?' I started to ask.

Perry interrupted my question. 'We just knew. We read it in the moonlight; it guided us here to this place. We knew you were on the moon, we saw the window open and close, and waited for you to arrive, but you didn't.'

'We came the same way,' Diana said.

'To the moon?' I asked.

'No. That's the strange thing,' Perry said, 'we came through the moon's window and straight to the Earth.'

'Why didn't I?' I asked.

'We don't know,' they answered in unison.

'Why didn't you go back?' I said.

'The way back had closed. We reckon the solar activity of the Earth's sun interferes with the stability of our window,' Diana explained.

'Yes, it's pretty unstable at the moment,' Perry added.

'I-I was at h-h-home, and then I was on the m-m-m-moon, but I don't know h-how long I was st-stuck t-t-there.' My teeth were chattering with cold.

'Come on, son,' Perry said, 'let's take you home.' He picked me up in his arms and carried me up the beach.

Diana started to sing...

The boy whistled a tune as he dropped from the moon,
he fell at such pace, far out into space,
he travelled so far, past many a star,
it happened so quick, 'til he dropped like a brick,
into an ocean, on a world of emotion.
This wasn't the end, he was found by a friend,
and though he would grow, he would always know,
when the moon was fat, the place to be at,
was by water wet, where he wouldn't forget,
the wish he unfurled, for the path back to his world.

Chapter 8

Time to Leave

'EVIE. FIVE MINUTES AND IT'S TIME TO BE OFF.'

Henry Briggs voice called from the bottom of the stairs, and stampeded into Eva's bedroom, where she stood looking out of the open window. Now devoid of curtains, the window looked bare. A breeze carried in the deep, throaty roar of the GETYOUTHEREFAST removal van as it pulled off down the road, loaded with all the non-essential stuff, like furniture, and ornaments, which were to be placed in storage until the new house was fixed.

The pale blue walls of her bedroom now appeared faded and empty, darker blue patches showing the original colour where her posters of the phases of the moon, crescent, half, gibbous and full, once hung.

It had only been a fortnight ago that the room had been full of her friends for a farewell sleepover, and to celebrate her reaching double figures. They had made it a special tenth birthday, with lots of chocolate cake.

She remembered the presents from her friends. They'd given her bars of her favourite 85% chocolate, the dark fair-trade stuff, which came from exotic places like Ecuador, Costa Rica, Ghana and Dominica. She had once looked in an atlas to see where in the world these places were, which helped her in geography lessons. It had come as a surprise to her friends at school, that chocolate came from trees growing in such far off places, as most just thought it came from the local supermarket.

Another gift was a book, all about the moon, from Mrs Piper, her favourite teacher.

Then there was a pair of water wings from Aunt Dora, with a note, saying, 'to help you stay safe in your new home by the sea, at least until I can come and visit;' the gift came with a ten pound note, a pound for each of her years. This was typical of her aunt, who'd always had an inflated sense of humour and a heightened sense of mischief, much to the annoyance of her brother, Henry.

She would certainly miss them all, but as her father had intoned, 'think of all the new friends you'll make, and when we're settled, perhaps some of the old ones will visit.'

Outside, the sky was clear and blue. Her gaze lingered on the ghostly shape of the moon, as it dared to show its face against the cobalt sky.

For a moment, she was sure the man on the moon was watching her, and she remembered the surprise of seeing the moon through the telescope her mum and dad had bought for her birthday, three years ago. Her father had set it up in the exact position she now stood in.

Yesterday, he had carefully dismantled it and packed it securely away in an old blanket and lots of bubble wrap, the big kind, which popped loudly, before loading it into the back of the newly acquired van, along with the last remaining boxes of stuff they would need in their new home.

Eva thought back to the beginning of the year, when her father had reluctantly accepted redundancy from his job at the college. She recalled the numerous times she'd suddenly woken, to hear the muffled sound of her parents voices through the wall separating their bedrooms, as they talked deep into the night, wondering what to do for the best.

Then unexpectedly, one nameless evening, while she was

with her father, playing games on the computer, and her mother was at work at her part-time job in the local shop on the corner of the street, the phone had rung.

The one side of the conversation she heard went something like...

'Come again...what...let me get this right...he's putting it up for sale...not on the market yet. Yes, Derek...thanks for calling...It's something to think about...No, I won't leave it too long... thanks again. Bye.'

It turned out that Derek was head of the woodwork department at the college where her father used to work. He owned the little cottage they had stayed in when she was five.

The next day, Eva's parents had shot up to the coast, leaving the girls in the care of Henry's sister, Dora.

Dora was a couple of years older than her brother, Henry, and definitely not the sensible one. She, like her niece, Eva, had a fascination with all things to do with the moon.

Her short, dark-brown hair was streaked with silver and gold highlights, and once, she'd had her head shaved, and a small, crescent moon tattoo placed above her left ear, similar to the one on her left wrist. Later, she'd had one of the full moon peeping out from behind a cloud, tattooed on her right hand.

Her mother had been mortified when she saw it, but her father just laughed, saying things like, 'she's like the moon, she waxes and wanes,' or, 'it's just a phase.'

Dora never did change. To the moon, she stayed true and loyal, which is more than can be said for her short-lived husband. She'd met a rock musician at a music festival. He played the bass guitar in a band, The Lunatiks, and together they wrote all the songs for the bands one and only album, which sold millions, worldwide. Every song had a mention of the moon somewhere within its lyrics.

Ten months after their marriage, on a beach in Bali, he went on a world tour and never came back. By the time the band reached Japan, they'd split up, differences in direction, the press reported. The last reports Dora had heard was that her ex was running a beach bar on an island, somewhere in the South Seas.

Dora hardly missed him. After the divorce, and able to live off the royalties of The Lunatiks classic album, she enrolled in several evening classes; creative writing, and a variety of art related courses, including pottery, which she instantly took to, festooning her pots with images of the moon in all its phases.

Henry called her arty-farty; her stock reply was, 'don't call me arty.'

After three days in Dora's care, Eva's parents had returned, with news of a new start.

With the house immediately placed on the market, so began a tense time of waiting for a buyer, followed by the obligatory survey, and more waiting, before the heated rush of packing, all the time singing the family's new mantra...fresh start, new beginning.

Waiting is never easy. There is always the niggling doubt lurking at the back of your mind...I should be doing something; I feel I'm going nowhere...as an unwelcome distraction, especially when you're pushing the boat in a new direction. When the waiting ends, everything speeds up, as the river's current sweeps you along on an unknown course, only the destination of this particular river was known, the seaside, complete with its uncharted waters.

Deep thoughts for a newly instated ten year old to manage, but they didn't have time to hang about in Eva's mind, as her father's voice rang out again.

'EVIE. GET DOWN HERE IMMEDIATELY. MUM JUST RANG, THE MONEY'S THROUGH. SHE AND FELICITY ARE HALFWAY TO THE COAST. SHE'LL HAVE A FIT IF WE DON'T LEAVE THIS INSTANCE.'

Eva sensed the tension in his voice, and waving to the moon, she closed the window, grabbed her bag from its vigil by the door, and raced down the stairs to where her father waited, impatiently juggling the house keys, Patch sitting by his side.

'At last,' he said. 'We've to drop the keys off at the solicitors, Dobson and MacReady, on the High Street, on the way.

Chapter 9

Heading for the Coast

The long drive couldn't decide if it wanted to take an eternity, or pass by rapidly, and with only a brief stop at one of the several services that lined the route, Eva decided that the journey was the latter. On the way, her father regaled her with information about their destination.

'Turnstones Campsite gets its name...'

'I know, dad,' Eva interrupted, 'from a bird...I've seen the picture in your bird book.'

'Well there'll be plenty of time to go birdwatching; there's a nature reserve nearby. We'll have to get you some binoculars. There's a brochure there,' he said, pointing at the dashboard.

Eva pulled out the leaflet from the glove compartment and opened it to a map of the area, showing Turnstones clearly. She could see that it sat at one end of Moons Bay. Amounting to nearly fifteen acres, the campsite stretched inland, from the sand dunes, sloping gently up to the coastal road.

The entrance area comprised of the cafe, a house, a couple of outbuildings, the boating lake and a crazy golf course. The rest of the site, a mixture of wooded areas and meadows for camping, also held several small holiday chalets.

Her finger traced a path from the cafe to the house, which was to be her new home, after the bit of work needed was completed.

'Why is the campsite closed, dad?' Eva asked.

'It's been closed for almost two years, except the cafe,' Henry explained. 'Bob struggled to keep it open, but it needs a bit of work. He had an offer from a big company, who wanted to rip it all down, fill in the lake, and develop it into a complex of high-priced holiday apartments; but he liked our offer better.'

'Because it was more money,' Eva said.

'Oh no, quite the contrary, it was less. He liked our plans to reopen Turnstones as a holiday site; you know, what we told you, with yurts and chalets as well as camping. Your mother has loads of ideas. I'm the one who has to carry them out though, so I'll need your help in the school holidays.'

Eva thought for a moment before saying, 'what about old Bob? Where's he going to live?'

Henry laughed. 'Always worried about someone or something, that's my little Evie,' he said, as he pulled into the outside lane of the motorway to overtake a caravan that was hogging the middle lane. 'Bob is going to stay living above the cafe; he's going to be working with us, as our handyman, until we get settled. After that, I believe his plan is to go off and explore the world.'

'Is he going to work in the cafe?'

'Why do you want to know? Is it because of his chocolate mousse?'

'It was nice,' Eva said, licking her lips.

'How do you remember that?' her father said, shaking his head in amazement. 'It was five years ago.'

Eva thought for a moment before answering. 'Well, you remember me when I was five. Who will run the cafe?'

'Mrs Friedman, from Nelsons Cove, is going to run it. Don't worry, I'm sure the recipe for chocolate mousse will be passed on to her.'

'Daddy,' Eva said, a little anxiously.

'Yes, dear,' Henry said, casting a quick glance in her direction, 'what's the matter?'

'The sign back there,' she said, pointing to a turning they'd just passed; 'it said, to the coast.'

Chapter 10

Welcome to Turnstones

Bob was waiting at the gate when Henry finally turned off the road. 'Welcome to Turnstones,' he said, obviously pleased to see them. 'Your wife arrived a good hour ago. She's in the chalet with the little one. I told her that the cafe's open. Hilda, Mrs Friedman, says it's always quiet on a Monday, and you're to eat there when you're ready.' He then waved them through in the direction of the chalet, their temporary home until the work on the house was finished.

Henry hardly had time to draw breath before he was moving boxes into the chalet. Eva was told to take Patch for a walk, while Felicity climbed into the front seat of the van and fell asleep.

After several laps of the boating lake, Eva returned to find the van empty, except for her sister, still asleep. Inside, she found her mother hard at work cleaning the kitchen area, while her father was running feverishly around with the vacuum cleaner. Eva peeped in the bedroom, which she was to share with her sister, at least until the third bedroom was emptied of the boxes hastily stacked inside.

It was only when Felicity appeared, refreshed from her sleep and complaining of hunger, that her parents decided enough was enough, and they all traipsed over to the cafe where they were treated to the scrumptious meal Mrs Friedman had waiting. By the time they'd finished, the sky had clouded over, and all they wanted to do was go to bed.

Joy, who was never too tired to tuck her children in with a bedtime story, told the one about the cow who jumped over the moon.

Although Eva had heard the story many times, she was glad to hear its familiar words in this new place. She loved the rhyme about the man on the moon, and even though she knew the moon wasn't made of cheese, she still believed he lived there, and wondered just how he managed to survive.

Much later, Eva lay awake, listening to the unaccustomed sounds. Apart from her sleeping sister's quiet breathing, she heard the wind playing with a branch, brushing the sand off the roof, and a fox barking in the distance. Straining to dissect the sounds, she was sure she could hear the far off crash of waves on the beach, and hoped with all her tired might that she could go down to the beach in the morning.

With that thought, she drifted off into a wistful dreamy sleep.

Chapter 11

Eva's Dream

In her dream, Eva stood on the beach, watching a girl asleep in bed. The sleeping girl was dreaming also, her eyes flickering from side to side behind her closed lids, her nut-brown hair cascading over the pillow, its ends caught by the gentle breeze blowing in from the sea. Why the girl was asleep in her bed on the beach, Eva couldn't say, and anyway, it didn't really matter, dreams are like that.

'COOOOEE.'

The voice resonated through the air, and Eva looked up to see a colourful figure nestled in the crook of the crescent moon. His lustrous, golden eyes turned towards her, and waving, he leapt to his feet, hastily jammed his shirt back inside his trousers, and quickly buttoned up his emerald and ruby coloured jacket.

Out of a pocket, he pulled a tall, blue, stovepipe hat, which he set at a jaunty angle on his head, before scrambling up to the top of the moon where he began to dance a merry jig. Bright glittering stars flew out of his fingertips, whirling around his head before arcing their way down towards the Earth.

Eva thought about waking the sleeping girl, to warn her about the dazzling stream of red and yellow stars, to say about the green ones, the blue and purple ones, falling towards her.

But before she could, the first star touched the rich blue duvet covering the girl, and as it did so, a book mysteriously appeared; written on its cover, in big letters, were the words,

THE MAN WHO LIVED ON THE MOON. The book flipped open, and picking it up, Eva began to read the introduction...

So here I am, ready to write down my story, for you, my synergistic friend, wherever you are. I know you are out there in this world, I have sensed you, even caught a glimpse of you. You are my hope. I have travelled this globe searching for you, done all I can to find you and now I can only wait. I can only shine my light, and trust that it will lead you to me.

I will write down my story with the conviction that when you read my words you will feel the truth of my life wrapped in each letter, sentence, and chapter. By bringing my story into this world, I know its spirit will seek you out, the one who can help me find the reason I am here; only then will I discover my purpose.

Where do I start? What do I say? I can find no beginning, just a continuation, a line leading me, and if I think about it, probably to where I didn't want to go, but needed to go anyway.

Eva turned to the first chapter...

My name is Sessil, and there is a moon on my world, too; perhaps that's why I'm now continually watching yours, always waiting for a glimpse through its window, looking for the way back home to my world.

There are many stories about the moon on my world, as there are here, of how it affects people. Some profess that its light instils a feeling of melancholy. Myself, well I've always loved its light, whether it's the cool silver face it shows, or one with the golden glow. I love the colours in its aura, shining through the veiled curtain of cloud. On my world, night was the time for work, the hot days for sleeping...

The sound of an owl hooting woke Eva with a start. She sat up, bleary eyed and disorientated. Anxiously looking around the room, her eyes widened; she wondered where were the pale blue walls, adorned with her treasured posters of the phases of the moon. Where were the shelves that supported her collection of soft cuddly toys, and the cupboard overflowing with stuff she hadn't looked at for years, but her mother was saving for Felicity. Then she remembered; it was all gone. All she saw was the dark knots and swirling grain of the pine cladding of the walls.

She glanced at her sister's sleeping form, under the poppy-patterned duvet, on the other side of the room, and flopped back down. Something hard and sharp jabbed into her shoulder blade. Eva sat up instantly, and grabbed the offending item. It was a book, its dark indigo cover dotted with silver stars, and under the title, THE MAN WHO LIVED ON THE MOON, a golden crescent with a figure nestled in its perfect curve.

Eva was amazed. It was exactly like the one in her dream. Turning the book over in her hands, she wondered if her mother had bought it for her as a surprise, and tucked it under the duvet. The lure of the story soon chased all thoughts out of her head. She flipped it open to the first chapter...

My name is Sessil, and there is a moon on my world, too; perhaps that's why I'm now continually watching yours, always waiting for a glimpse through its window, looking for the way back home to my world.

There are many stories about the moon on my world...

Her mind whirled with delight. Too excited to read it all, she flipped through its pages, wide eyed at the clear script. Written by a hand that tried to keep to straight lines, but failed, it flowed from word to word, sentence to sentence. Her eyes lingered over the finely painted illustrations, particularly one showing strange domed, glasslike structures, tall, short, wide and narrow. People appeared to be rushing from dome to dome. One towered above all the rest. Inside this dome, she could see a tree, with tiny, antlike figures scattered around its base, while others seemed to be flying around its canopy of large oval leaves, painted in a variety of purples. Descriptions of the picture told of The Heartoak.

With her excitement calming down a little, Eva returned to the beginning, and read the chapters on how Sessil had fallen onto the moon, followed by his description of his fall to Earth. Having read enough, Eva was unable to get back to sleep, so she ventured out into the kitchen, where her mother was in the throes of burning toast.

'B#####, b#####,' her mother cried, which to Eva's tender ears, sounded like, bother, bother.

'What's wrong, mum?' Eva asked.

'Oh, Eva, it's you. Sorry about that. It's this gas grill; I'm not used to it.'

'Not used to what?' Eva's father asked, as he walked in from outside, with milk, eggs and a box of cereal.

'Henry. Where have you been?' Joy asked.

Henry winked at Eva. 'I've been looking for the fire

extinguisher,' he said, with a smile. His wife slapped him playfully on the arm, and started laughing, the tense kind of laugh that spoke of doubt and fear.

'Oh, Henry, have we done the right thing, coming up here, uprooting the children,' she whispered.

Eva, overhearing, spoke first. 'Of course you did, Mummy. It's like a big adventure, and I know it's all a bit strange, but I'm sure we'll all be all right. Anyway, I can't wait to visit the beach and explore. And daddy promised to buy me a pair of binoculars so I can watch the birds. I heard an owl hooting...' Eva's words tailed off as her mother's arms wrapped around her. Henry joined in, for a group hug.

At that moment, Felicity walked in, yawning. 'I can smell breakfast, is it ready?' she asked, and they all settled around the table for cornflakes, eggs, orange juice, and promises of a walk on the beach later that afternoon.

Chapter 12
Old Bob

Eva spent half-an-hour unpacking a few boxes in her bedroom, with no help from her sister and Patch, who played tug-of-war with her books and toys. When she complained, her mother suggested taking the dog out, to run a bit of steam off him. Glad of an excuse to get away from Felicity, Eva set out to explore the campsite, Patch running ahead of her as she veered towards the boating lake.

Patch started running round in circles, barking at the sky, and Eva looked up at an aeroplane, a shining silver bird with a long vaporous tail, streaking across the blue sky. He suddenly went quiet, when he spied a figure sitting on a bench on the far side of the boating lake, staring into its shallow waters. Patch's head and shoulders dropped low, and with his tail held straight out behind, he moved forward, a hunter stalking his prey. Eva hurried after him.

The figure glanced up, Patch rushed forward, barking in recognition. Bob stretched out a hand, as Patch, his tail wagging franticly, welcomed a scratch behind his ears.

'Used to be much cleaner,' Bob said, glancing up as Eva drew level with him.

She gave him a puzzled look.

'The lake, not the dog,' Bob said, chuckling. 'Friendly fellow for all his bluff,' he added.

Eva nodded in agreement. 'I'm sorry if he barks too much. It's just that he doesn't like aeroplanes.'

'Me neither,' Bob said. 'I remember you. You're the little one who loves dark chocolate. Must be four or five years ago when you first turned up. Had fish fingers and my chocolate mousse, if my memory serves me right.'

'Urrgh,' Eva said, pulling a face. 'Not all together,' she added, in all seriousness.

Bob laughed at her expression. 'No; that'd be awful.' He turned to stare into the water of the boating lake. 'Not as clean as it used to be, and it's drying out. Years ago it was connected to the big lake by a small stream. Nothing flows anymore; well, only a trickle, enough to keep it wet.'

'Another lake,' Eva said in surprise. 'I didn't see it yesterday, when I took Patch for a walk.'

'No, you wouldn't,' Bob said, 'unless you know what you're looking for. It's all overgrown; trees, reeds and bulrushes encroaching from every side. Hardly a drop of water in it these days, and that's smothered by water lily leaves, pondweed, and the like.'

'Where is it?' Eva asked, 'I'd love to see it.'

Bobs face lit up. 'You would. Well, come on, I'll show you.'

Eva followed Bob away from the boating lake, along a narrow path, one side lined with thistles that snagged at her jumper, the other side held the remnants of the stream.

'Only a few puddles, now,' Bob said. 'Course, when it rains you get a bit of a flow, but not much.'

The path wound its way inland, leading to the foot of a wooden viewing platform.

'Up here,' Bob said, leading the way up weathered steps, cracked and split by years of neglect, to the top of the platform, ten foot above the ground. 'Look.'

Eva could see the depression that formed the bed of the overgrown lake, over fifty yards wide and twice as long.

'We used to have fish in here. My dad filled it with trout. See there,' Bob said, pointing to an old wooden structure half-buried by an alder tree; that's the sluice gate, that's what controlled the flow to the boating lake. There's another gate at the other end, connecting the lake to Moon River, as it flows into the marshes south of Turnstones. Used to be kingfishers, herons, ducks, and come the autumn, visiting geese from up north. There's a bird reserve just down the road.'

Eva's face lit up with excitement. 'If it's fixed, will it work again?' she asked.

'Yes, but you'll have to talk to your mum and dad about it. It'll be lots of work, clearing the scrub growing in the lake. Look behind you.'

Eva moved to the opposite side of the platform. 'I can see the sea,' she exclaimed.

'Aye, you can. That's Moons Bay,' Bob said. 'See the little bit of land that sticks out, on the south arm of the bay.'

'Yes; it's curved.'

'That's Crescent Island. There's terns nesting over there at the moment.'

'Cor,' Eva said, wondering what terns were. 'I'd love to see them.'

'Best not disturb them. Your little chap, here,' he said, looking down at Patch, who sat with an air of innocence, wagging his tail, 'he'd be after them.'

'Why's it called, Crescent Island?' she asked.

'It's the shape. Curves like the moon,' Bob answered. 'Dangerous to get to. Tide flows pretty fast through the gap between it and the land.'

Eva only half heard his warning; her mind was fixed on the moon bit. 'I bet you could see the man on the moon there,' she said, almost to herself.

Bob smiled at his new young friend, saying, 'that you could. Bet you could back there, if the lake was cleared,' he said, gesturing behind them.

Eva's eyes glittered eagerly at the thought, as they walked back down the path, where Bob slipped into the cafe, and she returned to the chalet.

Chapter 13

A New Friend

Nestled in a secluded area, the timber chalet looked bigger in the daylight. Its cedar walls had weathered into a mellow tone that fitted perfectly into its setting among the trees.

A small garden ran around the building, and a glass and wood conservatory jutted out from the south side. Here, Eva spied her father busying himself at one of the windows. Whooping loudly, she raced in through the open door to see him setting up her telescope.

'Thought you might like it in here, until we move into the house,' he said, making the final adjustments to the tripod that supported the telescope.

The door leading into the open plan kitchen-living room opened, releasing an inviting aroma of tomato soup. Her mother's head appeared. 'Lunch is ready,' she said. 'Give Patch his biscuit, and come and eat while it's still hot.'

'And not burnt,' whispered Henry.

Eva started to giggle.

'I heard that, Henry Briggs. Any more cheek from you and you won't get any lunch.'

'OOOOOOOOOOOOH,' Eva and her father both wailed at the same time.

Lunch was a jolly affair; Felicity spilling lumps of bread onto the floor, much to Patch's delight, but the afternoon walk didn't materialize, postponed by the arrival of Clem Friedman, whose wife, Hilda, ran the cafe.

Clem, a builder from nearby Nelsons Cove, had come to assess the work needed on the house.

Not for the last time, Eva found herself in charge of her sister. Warned not to stray from the campsite, they went off in the direction of the sand dunes, Patch trotting happily beside them.

'Can we go to the beach?' Felicity asked.

'No. Mum said to stay close to home,' Eva replied.

'But I want to see the sea.'

'You can see it from the top of the dunes,' said an unfamiliar voice, coming from up in the branches of a tree.

Patch jumped up and down around the tree, barking madly.

'Call your dog off and I'll come down,' the boy said, as he scrambled down and dropped to the ground. 'I'm Jake,' he announced, 'and you're the girls from the camp. I heard you'd arrived.'

'You've torn your shirt,' Felicity blurted, pointing to a two-inch tear on the boys left side.

'I snagged it on that broken branch up there,' Jake said. 'Mum'll sow it up for me, it's only an old one, used to be my dad's, but he says it shrunk in the wash. Mum says she's always patching me up. She did this,' he added, holding up his leg to show off a huge red patch above one knee.

'What are you doing here?' Eva asked, but she'd already guessed. He was the spitting image of Clem, the builder.

'My dad's talking to your dad,' Jake said, making a fuss of Patch. 'He's going to be working on the house. He said it's a bit run down, but shouldn't take long to get right. He's good at his job, is my dad.'

'Well my dad is going to be helping him,' Felicity chirped.

The boy laughed, running his fingers through a thatch of untidy hair that stuck out in all directions, specks of sawdust falling out as he did so.

'I've been helping my uncle in his workshop. He likes me helping him. Have you met old Bob?' Jake said, pulling a face.

'Yes,' Eva said, wondering what this strange boy was going to say next.

'Lot of kids at school are afraid of him, 'cos he's a bit odd, but he's all right is Bob. He's been here for years. My dad said he's very interesting to talk to. Knows a lot about all sorts of things, and he's a good worker.'

Felicity tugged at Eva's sleeve. 'When can we go and see the sea?' she asked.

Jake laughed, saying, 'impatient, isn't she.'

'She's five,' Eva said, as if that explained everything, 'and her name's Felicity; mine's Eva.'

'Come on, then,' Jake said, leading them into an expanse of grass-wigged sand dunes.

'That's the edge of your campsite,' Jake said, with a nod back at the tree line. 'The sea is over there,' he added, pointing over the dunes.

'I can't see the sea,' Felicity wailed.

Jake led them further into the undulating dunes, always heading towards the tallest one. Climbing to the top, he said 'There you are, Felis.'

In the distance, they could see the thin frothy line of the waves rolling onto the shore, the blue green waters stretching out to the horizon. Seagull specks, dipped and dived in the foam.

'Where do you live, Jake?' Felicity asked.

Jake turned ninety degrees to the north. 'See where the dunes meet the cliffs at the end of Moons Bay; that's Nelsons Cove. It's only three-quarters of a mile from here. I come here quite often, on my bike, to watch the birds.'

'What's it like?' Eva asked.

'It's quite big for a village,' Jake explained, 'There's Herrings Staithe, that's the harbour, and there's old fishermen's cottages. Dad says they're now mostly holiday homes for city dwellers, looking for the country experience, or gift shops selling coloured sand ornaments, or art and crafts. He says the real locals all live on the estate on the outskirts of the village, or have to come into work from Nelsons Market, that's ten miles inland.'

He glanced at his watch, saying, 'I'd better head back. Dad'll be wanting to get home.' As one, they turned back towards the trees, retracing their footsteps back to Turnstones.

Chapter 14

Finding Their Moonbeam

It took me a long time to get used to this heavy body, and even longer to find my feet, both mentally and physically. By that, I mean, realizing the gravity of my situation.

Thank goodness I had Diana and Perry, who looked after me, helping me adjust to my new home. They took me back to their little sanctuary, in a corner of the country, where they managed to live, unnoticed.

Initially, I struggled to keep my colour; I found this body heavy and awkward. I longed for the lightness of my true self. Diana and Perry became my substitute parents, although other people knew me as their grandson; they were a lot older than I was, so it made sense.

With their help, I learned to keep hold of my colour. I was able to shed my physical form when the moon was out, and together, the three of us would skip over the moonlit water, searching for the moonbeam; the one tuned to our colours, which would enable us to return home.

They didn't find theirs for a long, long time, until, after a particularly nasty run of stormy weather, in the dead of winter, the clouds finally dispersed, leaving a starlit night sky.

The wind had stopped blowing, and a bright moon shone at its fullest. I watched as they pirouetted over the surface of the water in a flurry of silvery delight. Suddenly Diana cried out, a cry of joy, of excitement, of relief; Perry skipped over to her and took her hand, their colours blended perfectly.

I wondered why I hadn't noticed that before, after all, they'd told me many times how they'd come to this world together, by wishing their way to their moon, and falling through its window. Many times they'd recounted their surprise at falling into this world, a world so familiar and yet so different; as I was finding out.

I watched and waited, as two became one, in complete harmony with each other. They looked across at me and waved as they pointed at the moon. I saw a moonbeam lance towards them; it was exactly the same shade of silver as they were. I knew instantly it was for them. The spear of light touched their open hands; they began to rotate, spinning faster and faster until they were a blur of silver. The air around them hummed with colour; reds, blues, yellows and greens, blending into white; and suddenly they were gone.

I looked up at the moon, and for a moment, a microsecond, I felt I saw a curtain open and close. In my heart, I knew that they had reached their home.

As I slipped from my physical form onto the water, tears

filled my eyes, spilling down my cheeks, in a mixture of joy and sadness. I let them fall, as I whirled and twirled from ripple to ripple, my toes feeling the moonlight.

My colours sang of life, unfettered by the aggravations of this world, and as I danced, they grew stronger and brighter, reminding me, that however grounded I was to the Earth, in this moment of my life, my colours were my true reality. I knew with all my soul, that one day I would find my light; the one that would guide me back home.

I was alone again. It would have been easy to give up, and sink into a depression of blackness, but I thought of Diana and Perry, and everything they had taught me. Armed with that knowledge, I set off from my adopted home to begin a new stage of my life.

Chapter 15

A Secret Comes to Light

Diana and Perry had told me that they believed there were many like us, from other worlds, living quietly on the Earth. I've never met anyone else in all the years since they found their moonbeam.

Alone, I took to wandering the land. At every opportunity, I'd slip into my true self, and scour the moonlight, whether on the sea, a lake, or river, searching for my ray of hope, the one that would take me home; but to no avail. I learnt a lot about how not to be noticed, assuming various names, like Tom, Dick and Harry, coupled with numerous surnames, Grey, Brown, Green; people do like you to have a surname.

Eventually, tiring of forever moving, searching, I settled down and found work with a nice couple of Earth people, Archibald and Ruth, in a quiet location, and tried my best to slip into obscurity. No one knew who, or what, I really was.

Local residents called me eccentric, slow on the uptake, or just the village idiot. The titles became my camouflage.

Over time, Archibald and Ruth discovered my secret; they were moon watchers, and one night confronted me after seeing me on the water. I can still recall the conversation that followed...

'My boy,' Archibald said, 'we thought it strange, the aura you cast.'

'Yes. It waxes and wanes in tune with the moons cycle,' Ruth cut in.

I'd looked at them, aghast at being discovered.

'Don't worry, your secret's safe with us,' Archibald said, reassuringly.

'How did you know?'

Ruth smiled. 'It's in your face,' she said.

'My face.'

'Yes, your face,' Archibald said. 'It appears to get fatter as the moon heads towards its full phase, and leaner as the moon gets smaller.'

They then explained how they loved the moon; they'd even met in the moonlight, when it was full. That's why they moved to the countryside, away from the light pollution of the towns and cities, so they could stroll beneath a canopy of stars, and dream of winging through the heavens, visiting each constellation.

They knew a host of tales about the moon, and had shelves of books, each holding stories, such as the childhood ones of the man who lived on the moon, feasting on cheese, to more grown-up ones of star-crossed lovers, through to ones of werewolves and such.

Gradually they coaxed my story out of me, not to add it to their collection, but to see if they could help. They asked me to write it down for them; so I began, keeping my Earth name out of it.

They were happy years. Sadly, they both passed away, within days of each other, both aged ninety-one: old for this world, but young for my own. I hoped they'd found their heaven.

Archibald and Ruth were a popular couple in the village near to our home, and most of the villagers turned out for their funeral. I brought their ashes back to their home and scattered them in the woods, close to where I'd planted the five Heartoak seeds.

I wondered what I was going to do, until I had a visit from their solicitor, Mr Dunne, of Monks and Hood Solicitors, who informed me that Archibald and Ruth had left everything they owned to me.

Suddenly I was the owner of a property and a thriving business, which I continued running, as I had done for several years, due to their slower pace.

I saw the place as my own little dome against the wiles of the world, and often found myself under the thickening branches of the young Heartoaks I'd planted; they were growing at an amazing speed.

Seeing them, reminded me of where I'd come from, my world in the dome of The Heartoak, and wondered if my parents were still alive, after all, I had no idea how long I'd been away. I wondered if they'd given up on their little boy.

Inside, I was still that little boy, even though age had thrown a blanket over me. My body seemed older than my years, and I found myself beginning to accept my lot in life.

My searches for my moonbeam became less frequent. I realized that I was succumbing to the lushness of this world, and resolved to do what I could to help it retain this splendour.

I believed I was here for a reason, and if it were my destiny to return home, then it would be so, in the right time.

Chapter 16
The Friedmans

As July slipped into August, Jake would often accompany his father to the campsite, and after an hour or so helping, or as often as not, getting in the way, he would seek Eva out, and they would disappear to the sand dunes, or up through the trees to the lake.

It was here, late one morning, they found themselves sitting on the bottom step of the viewing platform.

'You'll be starting at the village school, come term time,' Jake said.

'Yes; my sister, too.'

'School's all right. You'll be in my class. Teacher's Mr Turner, he's all right. Have you been there?'

'Mum took me and Felicity to see where it was. We biked there; mum has a little trailer that fixes on her bicycle. She uses it for Felicity to ride in and to do her shopping.'

'School's in Market Street, at the other end from our yard,' Jake said. 'Dad says it's an odd name for the street, considering there's no market in the village. It leads all the way from the harbour to Nelsons Market. Then there's the church, as well as the school.'

Eva could picture Market Street, lined with its odd collection of houses and cottages, built of stone, flint, timber and red brick. In the older parts were little yards. Jake lived in one of these.

Only last week she'd followed her mother under a tired sign, declaring the yard to be that of Woodleigh and Sons, purveyors of timber, founded 1861. She'd leant her cycle on the wall under the window of the office, and sat in the shade, while she waited for her mother.

Woodleigh and his sons had ceased to exist long ago, and Jake's grandparents now owned the yard, selling building supplies and various bits and pieces of ironmongery. The shop occupied one side of the yard; opposite were workshops, where Clem Friedman and his brother, Zach, worked. At the back, wooden stairs led up to the family's living quarters. One of the windows had a cut out bird hanging from the top.

'That must be Jake's room,' Eva had thought. 'He told me all about the marsh harrier he'd seen flying over the nature reserve close to Turnstones.'

At that moment, voices had rung out from the shop, and a short, rotund man with wild, white hair emerged, carrying a box, which he secured in the trailer on the back of her mother's bicycle.

'Hello, little one,' he said, sitting down beside Eva. 'So you're Jakey's new friend. I can see you're a good girl, you keep him out of trouble for me.' From the pocket of his waistcoat, he pulled out a round tin and opened it, proffering it to her. 'Aniseed balls; haven't had them since I was your age. Found them in the new sweet shop in town, the one next to the art gallery. Here, take one.'

'Papa Friedman,' said an equally rotund woman, who had appeared with Eva's mother. 'You and your sweets; no wonder your teeth are few and far between. Do you want the girl to have no teeth? Look at her beautiful smile.'

'One or even two won't hurt,' Papa said, rolling his eyes. He leaned towards Eva and whispered, 'my wife, Bernice, she worries far too much. We've been together...' he turned to his wife and asked, '...how long, my love?'

'Too long,' she said, poking her tongue out at him. He burst out laughing; the kind of infectious laugh that spreads like a cold in a classroom of five year olds...

Jake's voice cut across Eva's thoughts, bringing her back to the moment. 'Who's that?'

The sound of voices drifted towards them. They scrambled up to the top of the platform, and looked out over the overgrown lake.

'Over there,' Eva said, pointing towards a clump of young willows. Three figures came into view. 'It's my dad, and yours, and Bob.'

'Wonder what they're doing,' Jake said.

'Let's sneak up on them and see.'

Creeping down as quietly as they could, avoiding the creaky plank two steps up from the bottom, they bent low, running through the trees and bushes, using them for cover as much as they could.

'So, Bob,' Henry said, 'you reckon you can fix the sluice gate, and get the culvert running back down to the boating lake; but what about the big lake, it looks empty.'

'It's just filled up with scrub,' Bob replied. 'It'll have to be cleared first; then see to the gate at the other end, the one that connects it to the river.'

Clem squatted down by the sluice. 'This'll need replacing,' he said, poking the rotten wood with a chisel. 'I don't know what's holding it together. Wouldn't hurt to replace the gate with a steel one. Cost you a bit, though.'

Henry rubbed his chin as he mulled it over. The lake had been on his list of priority jobs, but the work already completed was draining his funds.

'I'll pay for it,' Bob said, unexpectedly.

'No, you can't do that,' Henry said, amazed at the offer.

'Yes I can, it's my money, and I'd like to do it, before I go. This was always one of my favourite spots. It'd be nice to see a bit of open water again.' He paused, giving Henry a look that defied him to argue.

'Clem, you work out what we need, and get your brother to organize the timber,' Bob said, 'and I'll get the smith to make the gate. Agreed.'

After a minute or two of silence, Henry and Clem nodded in agreement.

'Good. Then I'll start on the scrub tomorrow,' Bob said, and casting a glance back over his shoulder added, 'and you two, behind that hazel tree, can give me a hand,' at which Eva and Jake sheepishly crept out from their hiding place, much to the amusement of the three men.

Chapter 17

The Domes of Feenix

As I've stated in a previous chapter, I fell from the moon, and landed here as a child. On my world, I had been a dozen or so cycles away from my transformation, when I would have been ready for the Synergism, the entwining of souls, linked by a common purpose.

I would have learnt how to master time, and slip into an ageless existence. Instead, my curiosity had brought me here to Earth, where time matters. Here, my body may look to be aging, but the essence of me keeps me young.

Diana and Perry understood this, and had done everything to help me find a place in this world. They taught me the importance of the now, live the moment.

I needed that, especially after Archibald and Ruth had guessed the truth about me; they knew by writing my story down on paper, that maybe I'd gain a better understanding of why I was brought to this place.

This world has many similarities to mine, but also many differences. Here, I am often overwhelmed by the verdancy of the Earth, the intensity of colour that is all around me; the abundance of water, of breathable air, and I wonder how far mankind can push it until the balance tips, and it slides into a state similar to my world, one of advancement that walks hand in hand with decline.

There, our history tells of the long battle between fire and rain, when each strived for dominance, but could only work if between them they could strike a balance; and so began what we term the long cycle.

As the last season of rain was drawing to its conclusion, scientists and ecologists were preparing for the change in the cycle, gathering samples of fauna and wildlife as they usually did, when the fire unexpectedly blazed in earlier and stronger than it had ever done.

Fire took control, and hasn't relinquished it since. It was so sudden; not at all like the usual slow change over.

In what seemed a moment, many died, as the world turned into a land of ash and dust.

What seas remained, bubbled and boiled in the heat; the rest drained into the empty spaces beneath the earth, where long extinct reserves of fossil fuels had lain, in an age before the fire and rain cycle was the norm.

Those of us who survived, retreated into the domes to begin a new life, protected from the heat of the sun by force fields, as night became our day.

Let me tell you a little about the domes, which were the uppermost tips of giant spheres that insulated our lives from the heat. Domes within domes filtered the light deep underground, enabling us to grow and manufacture our needs from what the scientists had managed to gather before the fire took over. Here we existed; our top people searching for a way of restoring balance to our world.

So many times I have gazed at the moon, with a wistful longing for any sign of my world. I needed a glimmer of hope to lighten my dull days. It seems to me that your moon is my moon, but viewed from the other side.

Memories of my time trapped there fragment my thinking; they tantalize and frustrate me in equal measure.

Images of other worlds, strange worlds, haunt my dreams, both night and day. If I'm not careful, dark emotions drag me down into a place of gloom. Faces from my world mingle with faces from this one, and I strive to find my place in either.

If I sink too far, I dwell in the past, where my father's anguished look and my mother's desperate screams, drown out all other thoughts and feelings.

So I allow the queue of questions to fill my mind, such as...Why did I fall to the moon instead of straight here to Earth? Could it have been the fear of the unknown that caused my change of heart, which threw me off course? Why can't I find my moonbeam?

Sometimes, memories of my time on the moon will populate my mind, filling it with images of strange, unobtainable worlds, viewed through its window. They flash across my imagination and I relive them...

The edge of the window glows violet. I see white creatures flying across an amethyst sky, dappled with orange stars that blink brightly. The creatures are men, women and children, ripples of purple trailing behind them, as the slow, measured beats of their long, feathery wings carry them through the air.

More worlds roll by; worlds of light and dark, spheres of wonder, of water, of air, earth and fire, filled with all life. Lost souls, found souls, creatures of myth and legend; creatures long extinct from your world and mine, waiting for a chance to return.

How long it takes for this procession of weird and wonderful worlds to pass, I cannot tell; maybe it happens in the blink of an eye, perhaps it takes a lifetime. All I know is I don't see my own world among the parade.

Worlds in worlds, one after another, cast their light through the window; my face burns, then feels icy cold, my eyes water.

The parade of worlds slows to a stop; a soft breeze ruffles my hair.

I know I'm now energy, but a feeling of physicality overwhelms me, my eyes now ablaze with the mass of bright swirling colours singing to me, beckoning me, enticing me to leap from my perch, into their entrancing, hypnotic world. But then a voice calls from behind me. Turning slowly, I see the beginning of the eclipse that will carry me to the Earth.

From the window, harsh, grating words ring out, penetrating my mind with vicious arrows aflame with fear and doubt.

I turn back to the window; the beautiful colours have melted into an angry, muddy mess of shadows; grey shadows that bask in an aura of lost hope. Its mask has fallen from its face, I see the true reality of this world, pulling, tearing at every molecule of my existence, with a power I'd never encountered before.

I remember a day when Diana and Perry took me to a funfair. I stood for a long while staring at one of the rides. A merry-go-round, with snow-white unicorns, flaming red dragons, yellow-eyed basilisks, sharp-beaked gryphons and other assorted creatures carved from mans mythology.

The carousel began to move, speeding up, and soon the creatures melted in a blur of motion. I watched, absolutely enamoured by the endless stream of colour, so inviting and seductive.

If Diana hadn't pulled me away, I would've been sucked into...as we turned to walk away, I could have sworn it hissed. I glanced around, the carousel had stopped, and I was looking into the face of a hissing serpent.

As then, I can even now feel myself sinking into its malignant embrace.

The pull was strong, but stronger was the soul of Mother

Earth, as she spoke to me of love, trust, and purpose: how could I refuse her...

And I didn't.

Chapter 18

Unexpected Arrival

Autumn was well under way, and the half-term holidays just begun, when work on the house reached a conclusion, and Eva and her family were able to move in.

The next day, Eva and Felicity were playing by the boating lake with Jake. Both sets of parents were in the cafe, discussing plans for the renovation of a pair of old railway carriages. Henry had found them, rotting, on a farm near Nelsons Market, and they were due to be delivered soon, ready to be turned into holiday accommodation.

Their discourse was interrupted by the sound of a large vehicle driving through the gates of Turnstones. Rushing out to inform the driver that the site wasn't open, Henry was struck dumb to see his sister, Isadora, lean through the window of a battered old horsebox drawing up by the boating lake.

Eva and Jake ran over to peer through the window at the rear of the vehicle.

'I want a look,' Felicity screeched, franticly leaping up and down until Jake picked her up. To their amazement, it was jam packed with boxes, a few bits of furniture and a potter's wheel.

'Why didn't you tell us, Isadora?' a bewildered Henry asked his sister, after she broke the news that she'd sold her house, to a nice young couple with their first baby, and that everything she owned now occupied the back of the horsebox.

'I wanted it to be a surprise,' Dora answered. 'You remember, we talked about me coming up and converting one of the outbuildings into a pottery, back when you bought the place.'

'Yes, but,' Henry started to say.

'Well, little brother, if you don't want me, I passed through a nice little village a few miles down the coast...' Dora said, winking at Eva and Felicity, who had now joined them, along with Jake and his parents, Clem and Hilda.

Joy stepped in. 'Ignore him, Dora,' she said, 'he's having a bad day. Of course we want you to stay. What do you say, children?'

'Yes,' chorused Eva and Felicity; Jake joining in.

It didn't take long for the horsebox to be emptied, and for Dora's possessions to be stored into one of the outbuildings.

Offered the chalet to live in, Dora declined, stating that her newly refurbished horsebox contained everything she needed to be comfortable.

'All I need is somewhere flat to park it,' Dora said, with a smile, 'otherwise I'll keep sliding out of bed.'

Chapter 19

It's All in a Name

The unexpected arrival of Dora, who was, by her own description, a force of nature, meant that half-term was set to change into a busy round of fun.

The day after she arrived, Eva took charge of showing her aunt around the fifteen acres of Turnstones.

From the sand dunes, they wandered down to the nature reserve, and met Jake, who was watching a group of reed warblers. They even caught a glimpse of his favourite bird, the marsh harrier, as it skimmed the tops of the reed beds.

He joined them as they followed the little river through the meadow up to the old overgrown lake.

'Look, there's Bob,' Eva said, as they approached the viewing platform.

Bob was sitting on the bottom step, sipping from a bottle. 'Cold tea,' he declared, holding up the bottle. 'My old mother said it's good for me, it'd put hairs on me chest. Didn't work. Do you want a sip?'

'Urgh, no thanks,' Eva exclaimed, thinking about the hairy chest she didn't want.

'Dora,' Bob said, after being introduced to her aunt. 'Is that from Dorothy or Isadora? No, don't tell me, it's Isadora.'

Dora smiled at him. 'How did you guess that?' she asked.

Bob laughed and nodded at Eva. 'Little missy told me, and I've an interest in names and their meanings. Take Miss Eva Verity, that's life, and truth, even her surname, Briggs, has a meaning; dweller by the bridge. No bridges round here, unless you count the way over the old sluice. I'm working over that way on the new gate. You can see where, from up on the platform.'

Dora was amazed at the different aspects the platform afforded. Eva and Jake pointed out the sluice, and Bob explained the layout of the area.

'Years ago, long before my time, this whole area belonged to the church. There was an old abbey over towards Nelsons Market. When the monks left, it became the local manor for some rich lord. He built a house at Turnstones, as his hunting lodge. What's now the cafe and outbuildings were the stables. Course, the old house is long gone. The one Eva now lives in, is the latest to be built on the site.'

'So the big lake; did this rich lord create that, too?' Dora enquired.

'Yes and no. Natural dip in the land I reckon. Probably where the river used to run, but it moved long ago. There's gates at either end that were used to control the level.'

'The curve of willows and alders, that's the big lake,' Dora said, her eyes following the lie of the land.

'You'll have to clear the trees a bit, so the lake can fill up again,' Eva butted in.

'That's right, Eva,' Bob said, nodding in agreement. 'Shame that, but I've been planting plenty more over the years, even managed to get some special trees growing up near the small ponds beyond the lake. Anyway, better get back to work, the gate this end's nearly complete, and it's going to rain later.'

'My dad says you paid for the new gate, didn't you, Bob,' Jake said.

'That I did,' Bob replied, looking a trifle embarrassed. 'Paid for the gates myself. A sort of farewell gift to the old place.'

'Are you leaving?' Dora asked, as they set off towards the gate he'd been working on.

'Soon. Places to go.'

'Oh, Bob, why do you have to go,' Eva sighed.

'Yeh,' Jake said.

'I'm looking for something,' Bob said, shrugging his shoulders.

Dora smiled at him. 'Well don't waste your life looking for something out there, when what you seek is inside all along.'

Bob gave her a long look, as if trying to puzzle her out.

'I've been there,' Dora explained. 'After my divorce, I was lost; I spent a long time searching for a purpose. Thought it was out there in the world, but no, the answer was inside me. All my life I've wanted to work with clay and make pots, dreamed of doing it; lots of pots, decorated with the moon. It's made of cheese, you know.'

'No, Aunt Dora,' Eva said, 'It's a window. If you look through it, you can see other worlds. I read it in a book. There's a man who lived there, and he fell to the Earth on a moonbeam. I've seen him, he runs on the water when it's got moonlight on it.'

'You've got the book,' Bob said, quietly.

'Yes,' Eva said. 'It's called, The Man Who Lived On The Moon. I've read it. I don't always understand it, but the pictures are lovely. I copy them sometimes.'

'Mum said, when she started working in the cafe, she saw a book like that,' Jake said.

Bob looked thoughtfully at the two children; a look of sadness clouding his eyes that only Dora noticed. 'We'd better let Bob get back to his work; I'm sure he'd want to get it finished before it rains,' she said quickly, urging Eva and Jake ahead of her.

Bob nodded, whispering, 'thank you, Mrs...'

'Dora,' she cut in.

'Aye. Why don't you come back tomorrow, and I'll show you around the lake.'

'I'd love to,' Dora said, before she set off after the children.

Chapter 20

A Near Miss

Isn't it an undisputable fact, that the tomorrows often don't turn out as planned.

Dora spent the morning clearing one of the old stables, assessing the work needed to turn it into her pottery studio and shop.

Eva had to babysit Felicity, while her mother and father were waiting for the imminent arrival of the two railway carriages, and they were sitting outside the cafe, drawing pictures of Patch as he lay sleeping at their feet, when the first of the lorries, transporting the carriages, squeezed, with difficulty, through the gates of Turnstones.

Immediately they rushed off to where a crane stood waiting, ready to lift the carriage onto railway sleepers, laid out on a thick base. Quite a crowd had gathered to help. Jake stood alongside his parents, grandparents, and his uncle, Zach, talking to Bob and Dora. The task of settling the carriage into position went surprisingly smoothly.

With hardly time to step back and admire their handiwork, the second lorry arrived. This time, as the carriage lifted into the air, one of the guiding ropes snapped, the end whipping back and hitting Clem on the chest. He fell over, as the end of the carriage dropped towards him.

Eva watched in horror as her father and Zach pulled sharply on their rope, trying desperately to steady the carriage. The crane driver pulled at the controls in the crane's cabin, attempting to stop the downward thrust.

Everything happened in slow motion, or so it seemed to Eva. Suddenly, just as it appeared that Clem was about to be crushed, she saw a golden figure dive under the carriage and grab him, hauling him aside, just as the end of the carriage hit the ground.

Eva couldn't believe her eyes when she saw Bob lying beside Clem. He caught her eyes, and smiled knowingly, but she didn't have time to think, as Clem's family crowded around.

Thankfully, Clem wasn't hurt, and work to secure the carriage resumed. It was late afternoon by the time Eva's father called it a day. As the crane and the lorries departed, the group stood around admiring their handiwork, with everyone throwing in ideas on ways to renovate the two carriages.

Somewhere amid all the talk, Dora put forward the suggestion that as it was going to be a warm, sunny, autumnal evening, there should be a party, a celebration of the day. Cheers of agreement rang out as everybody headed to the cafe.

Dora found a few bottles of wine in her horsebox. Hilda produced some chicken and chips, and to cap it all, she brought out a large chocolate and coffee gateau she'd prepared for the weekend opening of the cafe. She muttered something about, as there weren't many visitors at present, it'd only go to waste if it wasn't eaten.

The buzz of their voices, accompanied the clank of forks on plates, and the chink of a bottleneck on the rim of a glass, suddenly quietened. All eyes turned skyward at the sound; a low fluttering hum, as patterns, like smoke, swirled and spun against the last melting colours of the sunset.

They watched in wonder at the spectacle, and suddenly it stopped. The black clouds dropped from the sky, beyond the trees, leaving a silence that hung in the air, broken only by an owl hooting in the distance. The bark of a fox sounded from the sand dunes.

'That's the starlings,' Jake whispered to Eva, 'they'll all be roosting in the reeds on the reserve.'

'Hey, you two,' Joy called, 'how about a hand clearing up.'

Eva looked at Jake and pulled a face, before they each picked up a pile of plates and carried them into the kitchen of the cafe.

Many hands make light work, so it's said, and in this case it proved to be true. Emerging from the cafe, someone mooted a walk to the beach was in order, which was agreed by all, but only on condition that there was to be no skinny-dipping, much to Dora's disappointment.

'Too cold,' voiced Bernice Friedman.

'No; too old,' said Papa.

'Never,' replied his wife, 'it's just that you'd need ironing first.'

Chapter 21

Good Evening for a Party

Once on the beach, someone found a pile of driftwood, obviously gathered to make a fire, but never used.

An almost full moon hung in the night sky, as Eva and Felicity, together with Patch, set off to look for more wood. Vibrant orange, red and yellow flames licked the evening air, as they returned, arms laden with driftwood and dry seaweed. Patch dropped a large stick in the sand, barking furiously when someone threw it onto the roaring fire; red flickering faces sat around, basking in its warmth.

Dora began to hum a tune, others joined in, attaching words to the refrain...

The man on the moon, does he whistle a tune,
as he closes the drape with a swish and a scrape.
I may be wrong, but it won't be long,
before he gives them a pull, and the moon's once more full.

Its beams shining bright, light up the night,
on the water they'll dance, with a skip and a prance,
and the tune he'll impart, will capture my heart.
The sweet refrain, will wash away my pain,
make me whole once more, with its wonderful score,
but it's gone to soon, back to the man on the moon.

The song ended. A warm silence followed. Someone threw a few more bits of driftwood onto the fire, which spat and crackled with delight at having more food to consume.

'What can you see when you look into the flames, children?' Joy asked.

Eva stared, without blinking, until her eyes hurt, and suddenly she saw something. 'It's a bird,' she cried excitedly, 'it's red and gold, no, now it's blue and purple.'

'I can't see it, mummy,' Felicity wailed. 'I want to see it.'

'Keep looking, dear,' her mother said

Eva took no notice of her sister. Instead, her mind became possessed by the dancing flames, as vaporous birds opened their wings and lifted into the air, chased by dogs who ran wild among the embers; people, dressed in the exciting fiery colours of the fire, twirled round and round.

A voice began to tell a story, breaking her concentration. It was her Aunt Dora...

Long ago, there lived a boy, who'd heard that the moon was made of cheese; not a soft cheese like brie or camembert, nor one as hard as parmesan. One evening, as the sun had begun to slip from the sky, he wished that he could build a ladder to the moon and see for himself what kind of cheese it was made of.

'I know,' he said, 'I'll go to the forest and find some wood to make a ladder.'

But there wasn't a tree tall enough to reach the moon. He was very sad, and cried a bit, at least until a large black and white bird landed on a branch just above his head.

Now the magpie is a mischievous bird, and he watched the boy for a moment or two. 'I know how you can get to the moon,' he cawed raucously.

The boy looked up, hopefully. 'How, please tell me how,' he cried loudly.

'Are you sure you want to know?' the magpie asked.

'Oh yes. I wish it more than anything.'

The bird's beak twisted into a smile, and he hopped to the end of the branch and jumped up and down a few times. Five acorns fell to the ground. 'Take these, and plant them in the meadow, and they'll grow to the moon.'

The boy gathered them up and ran to the meadow next to the wood. He looked at an oak, and sure enough, the moon sat on the uppermost branches of the tree.

He squealed with delight as he picked up a stick and made five holes in the soft grassy ground, before poking an acorn in each hole and squashing the earth back.

The boy sat down to wait for the acorns to grow, but he was tired, and it was past his bedtime and getting darker, so he went home, vowing to return the following day.

That night he dreamt of cheese, of using stars to grate the hard outside of the cheese, and then tunnelling his way through to the centre of the moon.

The next evening, he returned to the meadow to find five empty holes. A loud raucous cackle rang out from the forest. He looked up at the magpie, sitting in the lower branches of the oak tree; it was hopping up and down with laughter; how it was enjoying a joke at the boy's expense, until, that is, a shower of acorns fell from high in the tree, hitting the bird on the head. It soon stopped laughing and flew into the air, squawking madly.

The boy watched, and saw the bird touch the moon, which was, tonight, high above the tree, but this time he wasn't fooled. He knew who had taken the acorns. He'd been tricked, and promised himself that he'd do his best not to be fooled again.

'Good story,' remarked Papa Friedman, as Dora finished, 'good lesson too; not to be taken in by what you see, and what people tell you, always trust what you feel.'

'Dad,' Clem said, 'let's not get too deep. Why don't you tell us one of your tales.'

Chapter 22

Eva Tells a Story

Papa nodded. 'Well, ok, but we'll keep to the moon.' He then proceeded to tell the one of the moon being made of cheese, the cow who jumped over it, and the cat who played the fiddle, badly. Bernice joined in the telling of the tale; there weren't many words as they acted each part. Everyone soon fell about, laughing.

'What about you, Evie? You love the moon, especially the man who lives there,' her father said. 'Why don't you tell one of yours?'

'I-a-I,' Eva stuttered, aware that all eyes were on her. 'Well there is one from my scrapbook; I drew a picture of it. There was a moon, it was solid, not cheese though, that'd go mouldy. Dad likes the mouldy cheese; he calls it blue, just as I coloured this moon. Anyway, it was all sloshy inside, watery, and there were big fishy things swimming in it...'

'You sure it wasn't an aquarium,' Jake chirped up, 'everyone knows the moon's yellow...or silver.'

'Our moon is gold or silver, but this was definitely blue,' she said, in a tone that said don't interrupt, which everybody thought was funny, all except Felicity, who, snuggling in her aunties arms, had drifted off to sleep.

Her father launched into an out of tune rendition of the classic song, Blue Moon, and was quickly hushed.

'The moon was blue,' Eva continued, 'and when I saw a blue moonbeam, I caught it and zoomed up to the moon. It looked like a window and I thought I was going to break the glass, but I didn't, I just fell through into another world. It was all watery, but I didn't get wet. A big whaleylike creature swam up to me. I thought he was going to eat me, but instead he let me stroke his nose; it was soft and pink. I think it tickled, because he wriggled, and his pointy ears twitched, and his long whiskers went all wavery. Did I say he had whiskers that reached out further than my arms, and he was covered in ginger stripes.'

'Then he spoke to me. Bubbles came out of his mouth; his voice was very deep as he told me his name was Rumbel, and that he was a caterwhale. Then he let me hold his fin, and we swam up to the surface ever so quickly. The sky was green with pink stars.'

She paused and took a deep breath.

'There were lots of caterwhales, all different colours, silver, black, grey and brown, and lots of ginger ones that swam over to us. Rumbel said they were his family; his wife, Crimb, and seven children, Rumbell, Tumbel, Bumbel, they were the boys; Timbel, Crimbel, Nimbel and Rimbel, his girls. We swam, and splashed, and played a lot, until the sky started to go red.

Rumbel said it was time for me to go home, but I didn't know how. Then he told me to look up, and guess what I saw, a big yellow moon, and I wished for a moonbeam to shine down and carry me home: and one did. The end.'

Eva grinned as everyone clapped their hands together. Her mother leaned over and gave her a hug. 'I remember that one, Evie, you only drew the pictures last week.'

'I know a story,' Bob said. He'd been quietly listening to the happy gathering. 'It begins, once upon a time…'

'Not that old chestnut, Bob,' Hilda cut in. Everyone laughed.

'But all fairy stories begin like that,' Bob said, with a wry smile.

'So it's a fairy story,' Henry chirped. 'Not one with goblins, hob, mob or noblins.'

Bob waited until the laughter subsided before beginning.

Chapter 23

Bob's Tale

'In a far, far away place…' Bob paused for affect, 'there is a world of fire, a world so different to this one and yet so similar. Let me tell you about it. This world I speak of orbits a sun and has a moon, very like the one that we can see up there,' he said, pointing to the moon.

As all eyes turned to look at the golden orb hanging in the heavens above them, Bob carried on telling the story...

The people who live on that world don't respond to time as we do here on Earth. It has cycles within cycles. The hot follows cold, just like here on Earth, we call them seasons, but it also has a longer cycle; one of fire and rain.

How can I best describe it? Imagine if you will, a mythical creature, a bird of unimaginable beauty, clothed in feathers glowing with colours, not of the earth, or the sky, or the sea, but colours of fire, that is the world I speak of; a phoenix. In fact, that's its name, F-e-e-n-i-x.

There, the oceans are the brightest aquamarine, the skies, painted an intense cobalt, the earth, the richest reds and browns; but it all comes at a cost. Payment must be made to the cycle of fire, when the sun flames at its hottest, and the world burns.

The people on Feenix had to find ways to cope with the alternating long cycles of fire and rain. They evolved from beings of flesh and bone and blood. Now they are born of fire, still creatures of form, holding shape with their fiery heart, which from birth they must learn to control.

They must cool, enough to partake in the Synergism, a point in their lives when they blend with the soul of Feenix. Think caterpillar transforming into a butterfly, except of course the insect always remains physical. At their heart, a gleaming, bright soul, surrounded by a dazzling, colourful aura, that's held in place by an impenetrable membrane of amethyst fire.

As I said, this world is full of cycles; short ones, like Lumin and Dimm, think day and night; longer ones, of summer and winter, called Clement and Rime. In between these, are the Melt and the Nip, depending on whether the cycle is heading into the warm or the cold.

They've learned to live underground, and in domes on the surface, even in the time of the rain, but especially when the cycle turns to fire, when the sun burns hottest, and the surface turns to ash and dust.

They have knowledge, and understand that the surface will grow again, at least it always had, but that's changed; this latest time of fire has not been relieved by the rain. Something happened to put a spoke in the cycle. The seas are now dry, the land parched, and people's whole purpose is focused on finding out why, before they are brought to the edge of extinction.

All that remains on the surface is The Heartoak, an ancient tree, which, to the scientists' surprise, didn't burn. They put a massive dome around it anyway, just to be safe.

Two ecologists discovered, by communing with the soul of Feenix, deeper than anyone had communed before or since, that The Heartoak is the manifestation of his soul, crying for help. And yes, before you ask, Feenix is male. He informed them that the tree was sending out distress calls into the void of space, using the moon as a relay station, a window to other worlds. He showed them ways of tapping into his threads of colour, so they could look through this window, and see the many worlds he reached out to; not one responded, until Gaia, this Earth, called back...

Everyone was enthralled by his tale, except Felicity, who was snoring loudly. Dora shifted slightly and the snoring stopped.

Bob continued...

There was a boy; his name was Sessil, and he lived on Feenix with his parents, Holm and Red. He was young, growing towards the conclusion of his nurturancy, that's infancy on this world. His parents were caretakers of The Heartoak, and they all lived within its dome.

One bright, starless night, when the moon was full, I-he found himself ensconced in the lower branches of The Heartoak, happily night-dreaming. Moonlight reflected off some of the tree's seeds, and little sparks of colour made him think of the moon, and its window, and as he grabbed for the acorns of The Heartoak, I-he wished with all my-his heart for a glimpse through it, into those other worlds. That was when his wish came true.

I-he was at the window, and as I fell through, I grabbed for something to hold on to just before I blacked out. I woke up looking at your world; the blue oceans, the green lands, the swirling moist clouds of the Earth. I'd never seen anything so colourful. My world paled, compared to the Earth...

As Bob spoke, he heard someone throw a couple of pieces of wood onto the fire; casting a quick glance around the circle, he breathed a sigh of relief; no one seemed to have noticed his words slipping into the first person.

With her eyes half closed, Eva knew it was the same story she'd read in her book, The Man Who Lived On The Moon. She peeped across the flames at Bob. A strange golden glow surrounded him. She wondered if it was a trick of the light from the fire, and was about to ask, when she caught her aunt's eye, and knew that she'd noticed it also. The almost imperceptible shake of Dora's head warned her to say nothing.

Dora was glad Eva didn't mention the haze around Bob, but she did wonder if anyone else noticed it, and that he kept tripping over some of his words. She wondered why he seemed to be talking about himself, and made a mental note to ask him about it the next day.

Eva knew this story by heart, she'd read it so many times,

and as Bob came to the bit about falling from the moon to the Earth, she saw in her mind the little drawing that accompanied the words, but this time, her imagination saw its colours more intensely. She felt the desolation of the lonely boy: the sadness that would overwhelm him as he struggled with a new life on an alien world.

Chapter 24

The Party's Over

A tear fell from Eva's eyes. She raised her head and looked around the circle. She wondered if it was her imagination, or did everybody's cheeks glisten with moisture?

Bob sensed the melancholy feeling permeating through the air, and wondering if he'd gone too far, decided to finish the story: but it had no end. He looked up at the moon for inspiration, and for a moment, it seemed to pulse brighter.

An idea appeared in his head, and seamlessly he stitched an end to his story...

I felt alone...even though I found friends to help me. I struggled to keep my colour; this body was heavy and awkward and it took me a while to get used to it. I longed for the lightness of my true self. I learned to keep hold of my colour, by shedding my physical form, especially when the moon was full, to skip over the water, searching for the moonbeam, the one that would enable me to return home.

And it happened when Sessil least expected it. It was early morning, at the end of a grey, cloudy night. He wandered to where he'd planted the acorns from his beloved Heartoak around a small pond, so many years ago, and sat down with his back against one of the trees.

'You've grown well,' he sighed. 'I wish I could go home, I'd take you all with me.' The branches of all the young Heartoaks rattled in reply. He was sure they said, 'ok.'

A strange tingling ran up his spine, a whispering sound travelled up the tree and around the pond. A soft voice echoed through the air, shaking the branches. 'So be it, Sessil of Feenix.'

Acorns fell all around him, the water of the pond rippling with a delightful refrain...

The man from the moon, let him whistle his tune,
he's all alone, and wants to go home,
the time is right, at the end of this night...

As the last few notes sounded, they melded together, transforming into the figure of a woman, who floated in the air above the water. When she spoke, her soft voice carried the colours of the seasons. 'I am Gaia, the essence of this world, and you must take back all you have gathered; it is time for Feenix to rise.'

'But how can I return home,' Sessil exclaimed.

'With help, of course,' she said, and gesturing to the trees, a child emerged from the shadows and began gathering the fallen acorns.

Sessil recognized the girl.

'The one whose name means life,' Gaia said.

Suddenly, a shaft of light pierced the heavy mantle of cloud, and a moonbeam shot down onto the surface of the pond. He walked over to the pond's edge, and slipped from his physical form into his true self, gliding easily onto the water.

The girl watched the golden figure as he stood on the moonlit water, waiting for something to happen. She turned to Gaia, who smiled lovingly at her.

'You know what you must do,' Gaia said to the girl.

The girl began tossing the acorns towards the moonlight. They stuck to Sessil, forming a coat around his transparent body. Gaia waved her hands in the air, and all at once, threads of every colour imaginable appeared, carrying the seeds of the earth, sky and oceans.

'My gift for my beloved brother, Feenix,' Gaia said, and she promptly melted back into the air, leaving the remnants of a song...

> *It's the end of the night, the time is right,*
> *let the man and the moon whistle their tune,*
> *to take him home, no longer alone...*

Sessil waved to his friend, and gently took hold of the moonbeam. In an instant, he was gone; back through the window on the moon to his home, with everything he'd come for to help his world climb back on its cycle.

Bob finished speaking.

Maybe it was the emotion wrapped around his words, which affected the gathering; maybe it was the soft, silvery light of the moon, or the warmth from the glowing embers of the fire, that caused a thoughtful, almost melancholic feeling to descend upon the circle of friends.

The evening crept on, accompanied by a chorus of soft, splashy sounds, as the tide washed up the beach. The light of a ship, far off land, blinked, sending its reflection shooting straight into Moons Bay.

A sudden rash of yawning infected the circle, and Felicity slept on in her aunt's arms.

Chapter 25

A Walk on the Sand

Gradually the numbers thinned. The Friedman's departed, but only after Papa had drained the last of a bottle of wine, before bursting into a chorus of, 'Show me the way to go home,' after which he staggered off, threatening to drive everyone back to Nelsons Cove. Clem, who'd drunk orange juice all evening, took the car keys from him.

Bob, who seemed a little distracted and was lost in his thoughts, took his leave, and wandered off along the beach, Patch trotting behind him.

'Come on, Evie,' Joy said, 'I think it's time we headed home. Coming, Dora.'

'No. I think I'll stay a while longer,' Dora replied.

'Mum. Can I stay with Auntie Dora, just a little longer,' Eva pleaded.

'Well, young lady, it is getting late,' Henry said, after a little thought, 'but if Dora agrees...'

And so it was settled. Eva was going to stay with her aunt for the night. She couldn't decide if she was more excited by the thought of an extra hour or so on the beach, or by the prospect of a sleepover in the horsebox.

Hand in hand, Eva and Dora strolled down to the waterline, talking about the different stories they'd heard that evening. Eva showed her aunt the art of skipping stones, but only succeeded in creating ripples, and she gave up at the sound of Patch, barking, along the beach, towards Crescent Island.

'What's up, Patch?' Dora asked. The dog ran up to her and sat at her side, staring up at the sky.

'It's probably an aeroplane,' Eva commented. 'He's always chasing them.'

'No,' Dora said. 'Look.' She pointed in the direction of Crescent Island, at the tip of the curve that gave the island its name. Moonlight zigzagged straight towards them, across the top of the moving water and up the damp sand to their feet.

An eerie light hovered above the reflections, blurring the air; at its centre, a core of gold, in the shape of a person, a child, who held the sadness of the world in his eyes.

'It's him, Auntie Dora,' Eva whispered. 'The man from the moon; only he's a boy.'

'Quite so, Eva,' Dora answered, rather absently, as her mind carried her back into her past, to a time when she was a child...

It was late. They'd been travelling for most of the day, and now it was dark. With her father at the wheel, her mother sat with a map on her knees and a torch in her hand, navigating, and her brother, Henry, snored in the seat beside her. She stared out of the window at the mountain scenery, illuminated by a full moon.

The road skirted around a long glassy lake, its mirrored surface sparkling with delight from the light of the moon. It was then she saw the two silvery shafts of light, dancing on the moonlit water, blurring the air.

Suddenly, the moving, waltzing lights stopped, revealing two people, a man and a woman, clinging to each other, staring intently at the starry sky. A ray of light speared down from the moon. It was exactly the same shade of silver as they were, and as it touched their hands, they vanished in a blur of colour.

As the car sped around a long sweeping bend, away from the lake, she turned around in the seat to stare out of the rear window. She couldn't believe her eyes when she saw a golden figure skipping across the water to the place where the man and woman had disappeared.

No one believed her story. A trick of the light, a will o' the wisp, her father had said, but she knew what she'd seen; and now there he was again, on Moons Bay.

'PATCH.' Eva's scream brought Dora back to the moment.

'Eva, come back,' she cried, as she watched her niece racing after him. Fortunately, Patch had more sense than to try to tackle the fast moving current of the retreating tide, and he remained on the ragged waterline. Eva scooped him up, as Dora caught up with her.

'Don't scare me like that, Eva,' she said, giving them a hug. 'The water can be dangerous, especially in the dark.'

'But it's not dark, auntie,' Eva said, trying to reassure Dora. 'Look. There's the moonlight, and the man from the moon.'

But when they looked, they saw only the moonlight still skipping across the water; there was no sign of the dancing figure. Their eyes scanned the waters around Crescent Island, but all they could make out was a flicker of light along the beach; a minute or two later, Bob came walking towards them.

'Are you all right?' he asked.

'Did you see him?' Eva blurted. 'The man from the moon, he was on the water, out there.' She pointed out to sea.

Dora stared at Bob, her thoughts running wild.

He returned her gaze, and as if reading her thoughts, said, 'tomorrow; I'll be up by the ponds, beyond the lake. I always take a walk before the dawn breaks.' And he walked off, leaving Dora and Eva alone.

'Come on, Eva,' Dora said, after he'd disappeared into the sand dunes. 'It's time we went home; we have to be up early.'

Chapter 26

A Moonlit Rendezvous

Bob stepped out into the fresh morning air. It was early, and he headed in the direction of the lake. Moonlight still filtered through the branches of the trees, illuminating his way, as he passed the sluice gate and followed the path around the crescent shaped lake to the small pond, where he'd planted the acorns, when he first came to this place.

Sitting down, he pressed his back against one of the oaks, as he'd done so many times before, and sighed with relief as he felt as though he was melting into its trunk. He was always surprised at how fast the acorns had grown. They reminded him of The Heartoak, from where they'd come.

Closing his eyes, he allowed his thoughts to eddy around his mind. 'What am I going to say? I know they'll come; the child and the woman. Perhaps this is my time to return home; but my secret's been discovered before. It was, after all, how I came to stay at this place; what would be different now? The Henderson's, Archibald and Ruth, they knew; the child, Eva, something inside her has always known, ever since she first saw me, five years ago.'

Bob chuckled out loud. 'I couldn't help myself; there was water, lit by the moon, a link was formed, I knew I had to get her here; selling Turnstones was the only way. She's seen me since; two winters ago, on the frozen snow outside her house, and one spring, on the birdbath in her garden. Her name, Eva Verity, means life, and truth, and her family name; is she truly the bridge to guide me home, or perhaps the bridge to Gaia, the soul of Mother Earth. Maybe Gaia is the one who can send me home; just like the end of the story I made up last night, or did I make it up. And what about Dora, as soon as I met her, I noticed the tattoos.'

'That's because I've always dreamed of the moon,' Dora's voice sounded from the other side of the pond.

Bob watched, as Dora walked around the pond, Eva beside her. He didn't realize that he'd been talking out loud.

'Eva let me read the book you wrote; The Man Who Lived On The Moon,' Dora said. 'You left it in the chalet, so she'd find it when she moved here.'

'It was under my pillow,' Eva said.

'I know,' Bob said, 'you told me. I don't know how it got there.'

'Are you a wizard?' Eva asked.

'No. I'm just a soul, far away from his family, who only wishes to go home.'

Eva looked a bit downhearted by his admission.

'Magic is all around us,' Bob said softly. He waved his arms around him. 'It's in everything. These trees, I planted them as acorns from The Heartoak, the last tree standing on Feenix, but they grow here on your world: that's magic. On my world, we've lost it. Somewhere in our drive to evolve, in our stampede to be better, no, cleverer, than we were, we lost the wonder, the magic of life, and now we just exist to survive.'

'But can't you take some of our magic back to Feenix,' Eva said, 'like you did in your story.'

'I'm afraid, Eva, that that is just a story I made up, to stop me feeling sad,' Bob said. 'I've been here too long to hope of finding a way home.'

'I'll help you,' Eva declared, 'and Auntie Dora.'

'I certainly will,' Dora stated, determinedly. 'All I ever wanted to do, was find the man on the moon; ever since I saw the two silver lights catch the moonbeam, and you, on the water of the lake, when I was a child. Why do you think I want to do nothing else but make pots and decorate them with pictures of the moon? That's my hope, my wish, to see a lump of clay turn into something magical. That's my magic.'

'But...'

'No buts,' Dora said, 'I won't have it.'

Chapter 27

The Moon in His Eyes

Bob gazed at the pair standing in front of him, Eva mimicking her aunt, her face set with a determined look, legs slightly apart, hands placed firmly on her hips.

As Bob stood up, he laughed at the sight of them, and they both joined in. Their laughter rang around the circle of oak trees, shaking the branches, loosening acorns, which created a chorus of dull thuds as they hit the ground. The water of the pond rippled with a delightful refrain...

The man from the moon, let him whistle his tune,
and gather loose ends, say farewell to his friends,
he's no longer alone, now it's time to go home...

'Look, Bob,' Eva said excitedly, as she ran to the edge of the pond.

The moon positioned itself directly above the pond; its almost perfectly round shape reflected on the surface.

'I believe that's your moonbeam,' Dora said, holding out her hand and leading Bob to the water's edge.

Eva watched Bob, as he stood for a few seconds, gazing at the reflection of the moonlight on the water, before turning his eyes up to the moon. Its soft light bathed his face, deepening the lines etched there. She wondered how old he was.

As if reading her thoughts, he glanced at her, holding her gaze.

Eva saw the moon in his eyes, the irises, a perfect circle of gold, at their centre, a pupil, no longer black, but a fiery red. Before she had time to think, his body gave an almost unperceivable tremor; the lines of age on his face dissolved, each molecule of his physical being breaking down into pure energy, as he transformed into his true self.

Before her, stood her man, the one who'd lived on the moon, no longer old, but in reality only a few years older than herself.

Holding out his glowing, translucent hands, Bob took hold of Eva's and Dora's, and for a minuscule moment they too changed. It was as if they were inside out.

Their souls synergized with his; enlivened with images of Feenix, the moon, of his falling to Earth; images that lodged into the colours of their souls. But the imagery went deeper than his life; it stretched back into the origins of existence, when worlds communed with worlds, in a peaceful blend of balance and cooperation, jetting forwards into the possibilities of the tomorrows.

They felt the soul of the Earth reach out and take the hand of Feenix; saw him rising in a feast of greens and blues that softened the reds and yellows of the ash and dust. Birds soared and gyred through clear skies, animals drank from rivers that flowed through flower-filled forests into oceans alive with life.

'My brother; it is sad that you have had to endure a world under the thrall of time.' The soft calming voice spoke in whispers, which filled their minds with images of hope and reassurance as they floated outside of time. 'I have felt your despair, your yearning to return home, and that is why I, Gaia, the soul of this Earth and her moon, granted you the gift of being able to change your physical form into ethereal. How else could your blood, bone, and flesh transfer into pure energy? How else could you have danced on the moonlight?'

An image of Bob vapourizing into light and colour filled the minds of the three who were now one.

'And you, little Eva, and your soulmate, Isadora; it is your unwavering belief and faith in the man on the moon that has helped sustain Sessil in his times of doubt, when fear threatened to overwhelm him. It is your thoughts that have enabled him to fulfil his purpose of travelling from world to world. When he returns home, he will understand that purpose, and the years spent on Earth will seem but a heartbeat, compared to the time that exists on Feenix.

'So we do have time on Feenix,' Bob said.

'Time is a complex issue. Is it linear? Is it circular? Does it pass quickly or slowly? Perhaps it is just a matter of perception. We look to the past for our learning; we place our hope in the future, but can only live in the moment.'

With those words, the synergy dissolved, and Eva found herself hand-in-hand with her aunt. She glanced around; Bob was gone. Sessil was standing on the moonlit surface of the pond, conversing with a woman, whose green leafy gown seamlessly flowed into the water. Her earthy brown hair, streaked with ochre and purple, red and blue, glittered in the moonlight.

Gaia turned her face towards Eva and Dora, her emerald eyes

blazing with the richness of life. Her lips moved. The words, 'you know what you must do,' flowed towards them.

Together, they began gathering acorns and throwing them towards the figures on the pond; they stuck to Sessil, forming a coat around his golden body.

The woman held out her hands and beckoned to the earth, the air and the water. A myriad of colours, hues of intense depth, tints of extreme lightness, subtle tones, strong and delicate, wove threads of colour that melted into the coat that Sessil wore.

'My gift for my beloved brother, Feenix,' Gaia said, and she promptly melted back into the air, leaving the remnants of a song...

> *Let the man and the moon, whistle their tune,*
> *the time is right, let him shine bright,*
> *as he travels home, no longer alone...*

Sessil waved to Eva and Dora, and gently took hold of his moonbeam. In an instant, he was gone.

Eva clung to her aunt, a tear rolled down her cheek, not a tear of sadness, but a tear of joy. She knew her friend, who she'd only really known for a short while, but felt she had known for a lifetime and more, wouldn't be lonely any more: he was back home.

At Dora's urging, the two of them strolled slowly back down the path, to where their home waited patiently for their return.

Chapter 28

The Advantage of Going Home

Activity around The Heartoak was at a premium. The sudden and mysterious happenings had caused a storm of questions, that percolated the air around the heads of the cluster of climatologists, ecologists, meteorologists, dendrologists, and the host of other 'ists, who milled, like ants, scurrying to their queen, at the base of the tree.

'What's happened,' said one new arrival to the assorted 'ists. 'Where's the colour gone from The Heartoak?'

'Is it the end of the world?' another said, nervously.

'It must be his fault,' voiced a rather sour-faced individual.

'Whose fault?' several 'ists called out.

'The boy. The one who disappeared.'

'Where's he gone? And why him? He hadn't even reached

the Synergism.'

Conjecture and speculation, brewed a heady mix of bewilderment and anxiety among the throng. One second, the boy, Sessil, had been there; the next, he was entangled in a bright yellow thread, and then poof, he was gone, up into the heavens towards the moon. At the same moment, the mighty Heartoak had frozen, as if holding its breath. Its colour had drained away from its now glassy leaves, down crystallized branches, into the capillaries of its trunk and into its roots. The Heartoak was now see-through, transparent, empty.

A few daring 'ists, hovered around, poking its trunk and tweaking its branches, as if their actions would supply answers. All their prodding revealed, was that beneath a thin film of clear bark, was a gelatinous interior. What they couldn't understand, was that The Heartoak was waiting, and just didn't feel the need to make as much noise as the dumbfounded conglomeration gathered around its base.

In the cacophony of noise, a few people remembered to offer words of comfort to a distraught Holm and Red, over the disappearance of their son, Sessil, an hour ago.

That hour had passed agonizingly slowly, until someone

noticed that the mighty tree suddenly became animated; its transparent, papery leaves and crystal-like branches began beating out a rhythm, words emanating from the sound...

> *Will you all take heed, in our hour of need*
> *and look to the moon, make it quite soon.*
> *The cycle will turn, we'll no longer burn.*
> *Be ready, be steady, soon waters will eddy...*

The song echoed around the dome. The 'ists at the bottom fell silent and stood waiting, the air pregnant with expectancy. They didn't wait for long.

The first thing that happened, was a pinprick of intense yellow light at the centre of the moon, followed swiftly by an explosion of dazzling light. Out of the brightness, a golden sphere appeared, hurtling towards Feenix. It looked like a comet, complete with a tail. Long filaments, trailing in the wake of the sphere, lit up the heavens with colour, streamers of hot reds, oranges and yellows, side by side with cool blues, warming purples and steadying greens.

The Heartoak stretched and twisted; its glasslike canopy forming a nest in its uppermost branches, into which the golden sphere settled, its light giving colour to the translucent leaves.

The tree trembled with delight.

The sphere fragmented, and melted into the canopy of The Heartoak, whose core clouded over into a glowing, brilliant white. The watchers at the foot of the tree, speechless with fear, backed away, forming a wide circle around its base. Many dropped to their knees and began to pray, but the initial panic quickly gave way to curiosity, as the white pulsed with intensity, and the shape of a figure appeared inside the base of the tree.

Raised voices filled the air.

'Who is it?'

'What are those lumps clinging to its body?'

'They look like acorns.'

A hush fell on the assembled crowd as the tree changed once again. The acorns slowly began detaching themselves from the figure, and floated outwards, through the bands of colour that now filled the interior of the tree. They made their way through deep rich amethyst, that was closest to the core of white, flowed into a sparkling sapphire, travelled through successive bands of greens, yellows, oranges, and a variety of reds, until the now multicoloured acorns covered each fold of bark, twist of branch, and papery leaf of The Heartoak, forming little domes of colour.

At this point, the figure inside the tree moved, and a voice emanated from its hooded face. 'Come join with me in the synergism of truth. Let us, together, complete the restoring of the balance between the fire and the rain. It begins here and now.' The words echoed around the dome; the force field sparked and fizzed, crackling and splintering as it disintegrated, allowing the words to reach out to the world of ash and dust that was the surface of Feenix.

Collective gasps harnessed the surprise and wonder of the spectators, and whizzed around The Heartoak, as the coloured domes burst, and the air filled with the movement of creatures of all shapes and sizes popping into existence.

Two ecologists leapt aside, as a herd of huge black horses leapt from between the roots of the tree, the feathers at their heels waving in the wind as they galloped away. Mighty eagles and ghostly owls flew from the branches, alongside sparrows, wrens, swifts and starlings, all chattering and whistling with excitement.

Butterflies emerged beside dragonflies and beetles. Tiny spheres of colour rained down from the leaves of The Heartoak; where they landed puddles formed, and flowers and seedlings grew.

Some acorns floated into the air, where, high above the ground, they burst into clouds; rain fell, forming rivers and lakes that teemed with life. Creatures, large and small, ran, walked, tiptoed, hopped and cantered off to find their place in the new order of Feenix.

For all of the night and well into the day, the figure stood, unmoving, in the stunned silence of the muted onlookers, until all the acorns had dispersed. All that is, except for one small acorn of yellow, that melted into the figures heart; and finally, as the true colour returned to The Heartoak, the figure's hood fell back, revealing Sessil, who, with great joy and relief, stepped out of the tree into the arms of his parents.

He closed his eyes, at peace in the knowledge that he was home at last.

The End

About the author

Peter Basham has, from a young age, always painted. After a spell learning to be a chef, followed by years feeling imprisoned in a factory, making parts for food mixers, redundancy brought about a major rethink.

While searching for work, he stumbled into the art world, where he has experienced thirty years, selling his original watercolours and prints directly to the public.

With a small gallery, created at his home, he happily continues to paint, alongside his new venture, writing stories, suitable for young and old imaginations.

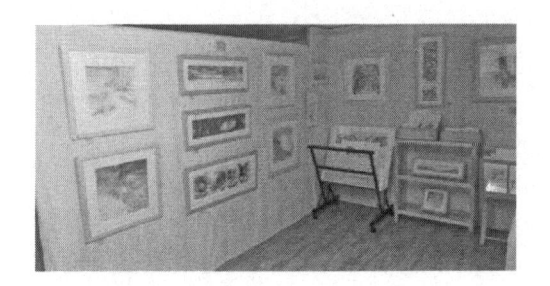

How Eva came to life

I have painted many pictures over the years, led on by my love and fascination for colour, in all its tones, tints and textures.

To see a blank piece of paper come alive with every brushstroke of colour, splash of water, and seed from my imagination, is a joy, but it came as a surprise, when one of those seeds, germinating in my mind, was one of words and the colourful feelings they can convey.

The result of that idea is my first book; The Man Who Lived On The Moon.

Having completed it, along the way learning many new skills, one of which was embracing the semicolon; I thought that finishing the story, seeing it in print, would be the end of my time with Eva Verity Briggs, and her fascination with the moon.

I was wrong. She wouldn't leave my imagination. She took me into another tale; The Blue Moon Of Hydros.

Although, The Man Who Lived On The Moon, stands as a complete story in its own right, the second book is being written even as the first is being published, and in it, we revisit Eva several years later, as she travels to a fantastical world that needs her help.